45 SHORT STORIES AND REFLECTIVE TALES FOR SENIORS

RELIVE THE MEMORABLE MOMENTS, THE LOVE, AND THE LAUGHTER THAT CONNECT US ON THIS SHARED JOURNEY THROUGH TIME

ALAN TURNER

Copyright © 2024 by Alan Turner -All rights reserved.

No part of this book may be reproduced in any form or by any electronic or mechanical means, including information storage and retrieval systems, without written permission from the author, except for the use of brief quotations in a book review.

Under no circumstances will the publisher or author be held responsible for any damages, reparation, or monetary loss due to the information contained within this book, either directly or indirectly. This is a strict disclaimer of liability.

Legal Notice:

This book is copyright-protected. It is only for personal use. You cannot amend, distribute, sell, use, quote, or paraphrase any part, or the content within this book, without the author or publisher's permission.

Disclaimer Notice:

Please note that the information contained within this document is for educational and entertainment purposes only. All efforts have been executed to present accurate, up-to-date, reliable, and complete information. No warranties of any kind are declared or implied. Readers acknowledge that the author is not rendering legal, financial, medical, or professional advice. The content within this book has been derived from various sources. Please consult a licensed professional before attempting any techniques outlined in this book.

By reading this document, the reader explicitly agrees that the author is not responsible for any losses, direct or indirect, that may occur due to the use of the information in this document, including, but not limited to, errors, omissions, or inaccuracies.

TABLE OF CONTENTS

Introduction	5
1. FAMILY AND RELATIONSHIPS	9
1.1 A Grandparent's Love	10
1.2 Love Letters from the War Front	12
1.3 The Family Quilt	13
1.4 Sibling Shenanigans	15
1.5 Dad's Fishing Lessons	17
2. HISTORICAL REFLECTIONS	21
2.1 The Moon Landing Watch Party	22
2.2 The Summer of Woodstock	24
2.3 The Magic of Radio	26
2.4 School Days and First Crushes	28
2.5 Memories of the Berlin Wall Falling	29
3. NATURE AND THE OUTDOORS	33
3.1 The Beauty of National Parks	34
3.2 Stargazing Nights	36
3.3 A Walk in the Autumn Woods	38
3.4 Seaside Retreats	40
3.5 The Secret Fishing Spot	42
4. LOVE AND GRATITUDE	45
4.1 A Love That Lasts	46
4.2 Acts of Kindness	48
4.3 Thanksgiving Traditions	50
4.4 The Joy of Giving	52
4.5 Letters from the Heart	54
5. SIMPLE PLEASURES	57
5.1 Morning Coffee Rituals	58
5.2 Porch Swing Conversations	60
5.3 Baking Christmas Cookies	62
5.4 The Charm of Old Movies	64

6. COMMUNITY AND FRIENDSHIP	69
6.1 The Local Diner Gathering	70
6.2 The Book Club That Saved a Life	72
6.3 Neighbors Helping Neighbors	74
6.4 The Reunion of Old Friends	76
6.5 Volunteering Together	78
7. CULTURAL TRADITIONS	81
7.1 Christmas Around the World	82
7.2 Harvest Festivals	84
7.3 Traditional Crafting	86
7.4 Celebrating Heritage	89
8. PERSONAL TRIUMPHS	93
8.1 Learning to Swim at 62	94
8.2 The Marathon Runner	96
8.3 A Grandmother's First Computer Class	98
8.4 The Home Renovation Project	100
9. PETS AND ANIMALS	103
9.1 The Loyal Dog	104
9.2 Cat Cuddles	106
9.3 Horseback Adventures	108
9.4 Birdsong and Serenity	110
10. MEMORABLE TRAVEL EXPERIENCES	115
10.1 The Road Trip to the Grand Canyon	116
10.2 A Train Ride Across Europe	118
10.3 The Cruise to the Caribbean	120
10.4 Visiting the Ancestral Homeland	123
Conclusion	127
References	131

INTRODUCTION

When I was a boy, I spent many afternoons with my grandmother. She lived in a cozy house on the edge of town, where the garden always seemed to bloom. One summer day, my grandmother and I sat on the porch, sipping lemonade. She told me stories from her youth, tales of adventures and mischief, of friends long gone and lessons learned. Her eyes twinkled with each memory, and I felt a deep connection to a past I had never lived but could vividly imagine.

This book is born from those afternoons on the porch. It is a collection of short stories designed to evoke memories, bring joy, and create a sense of community among seniors. My previous book, "Your Ultimate Retirement Adventure," explored how retirement can be fulfilling and exciting. This time, I wanted to focus on the simple, everyday moments and the special events that live in our memories.

This book aims to provide cognitive stimulation, emotional uplift, and social interaction. Each story is crafted to be relatable and enjoyable, touching on themes like love, history, family, nature, travels, and gratitude. These stories remind you of the little things that made you smile, laugh, and cherish life. They describe situations, events, and memorable moments in our lives that will probably make you think back to similar times. These stories are not fiction but come from my experiences or other sources.

The book is divided into thematic chapters, each containing several stories. Each story is designed to be read in one sitting, making it easy to enjoy if you only want to read for a short while. You can pick it up during a quiet moment, read a story, and then set it down, feeling a little lighter and a little more connected to the world. Or, of course, read many of them in a row.

Creating this book involved quite some thought. The focus is on positive, uplifting, and relatable content. I avoided condescending tones and complex plots to ensure the book is accessible and enjoyable for all readers.

You will find discussion questions and reflective prompts at the end of some chapters. These elements are designed to foster conversations and deeper engagement. They make the book a valuable tool for social interaction. Whether reading alone or with friends, these prompts can help you share your stories and reflections.

Writing this book has been a significant journey for me. I hope these stories will bring you joy, comfort, and a sense of connection. I aim for you to relive memorable moments, feel the love and laughter that connect us all, and share your experiences as you read.

So, dear reader, I invite you to join me on this journey through time. Let us relive the memorable moments, the love, and the laughter that have shaped our lives. As you read, I encourage you to share your own stories and reflections. Together, we can create a tapestry of memories that enrich our shared journey through time.

Thank you for allowing me to be a part of your day. I hope you find as much joy reading these stories as I did writing them. The adventure awaits.

1

FAMILY AND RELATIONSHIPS

One of my earliest memories involves sitting at my grandmother's kitchen table, the aroma of freshly baked cookies filling the air. With her kind eyes and gentle smile, my grandmother guided my small hands as I pressed cookie cutters into the dough. We laughed as flour dusted our noses, and she shared stories from her childhood that seemed like fairy tales to my young ears. In those simple, everyday moments, I felt an unbreakable bond forming, one that would last a lifetime.

Family and relationships are the heartbeats of our lives. They are the threads that weave our past, present, and future together. In this chapter, we will explore the profound connections between grandparents and grandchildren, the wisdom passed down through generations, and the comforting presence of our elders in times of need. These stories are meant to remind you of the love, joy, and lessons that come from these cherished relationships.

1.1 A GRANDPARENT'S LOVE

Grandparents have a unique way of making even the simplest moments extraordinary. On rainy days, when the world outside seemed dreary, my grandmother and I would bake cookies together. Her kitchen became a haven of warmth and sweetness. She showed me how to measure flour, crack eggs, and mix the dough with just the right amount of love. As the cookies were baked, we would sit by the window, watching the rain dance on the glass, and she would tell me stories filled with imagination and wonder. Her voice was like a comforting melody, and I felt safe and cherished.

But the bond between grandparents and grandchildren goes beyond shared activities. It is in the wisdom they impart and the life lessons they teach. I remember the day my grandfather took me fishing at the family lake. The early morning sun cast a golden glow over the water as we sat quietly, waiting for a bite. He taught me the importance of patience, of waiting for the right moment. When I grew frustrated with the lack of fish, he gently reminded me that some things in life cannot be rushed. His words stayed with me, shaping my understanding of perseverance and the value of taking time to enjoy the process.

Grandparents are also the keepers of family history. They are the storytellers who bridge the gap between generations. My grandmother had a treasure trove of tales from her childhood, adventures that seemed magical and real. She would explain the origins of family heirlooms, each item carrying a story of its own. There was an old pocket watch that had belonged to her father, a symbol of the hard work and dedication that had been passed down through the generations. Through her stories, I felt a deep connection to my ancestors, a sense of belonging that spanned time.

In times of need, grandparents are pillars of strength and comfort. I recall a particularly tough day at school when I felt overwhelmed and defeated. My grandfather, with his steady presence, sat me down and listened. He didn't offer quick fixes or dismiss my feelings. Instead, he shared his own experiences of facing challenges, reminding me that it was okay to feel vulnerable. His wise counsel provided a sense of reassurance, a reminder that I was not alone. During family crises, his calm demeanor and thoughtful advice guided us through difficult times, bringing us closer together.

The love of grandparents is unconditional and unwavering. It shines brightest in the small gestures, shared moments, and life lessons. They teach us to bake cookies on rainy days, fish with patience at the family lake, and find wonder in bedtime stories. They pass down their wisdom, keep family traditions alive, and offer emotional support when we need it most. Their love is a beacon, guiding us through life with warmth and understanding.

As you read these stories, I hope you are reminded of the special bond you share with your grandparents or the elder figures in your life. These relationships are treasures filled with love, laughter, and invaluable lessons. Let us celebrate the essence of a grandparent's love and their profound impact on our lives.

1.2 LOVE LETTERS FROM THE WAR FRONT

Picture a young soldier, not yet twenty, sitting in a dimly lit tent somewhere in Europe during World War II. The air is thick with tension and the constant hum of distant artillery fire. Amidst this chaos, he finds solace in a small piece of paper and a pencil. He writes to his sweetheart back home, pouring his heart into every word. "My dearest," he begins, "the nights here are long and cold, but thoughts of you keep me warm. I miss the way your laughter fills a room, and I long for the day I can hold you again." These letters were more than just words; they were lifelines, bridges connecting two hearts separated by miles and war.

The uncertainty and fear experienced by both parties were palpable. Every letter carried the weight of hope and dread. The soldier, facing the harsh realities of war, found comfort in imagining his sweetheart reading his words, her eyes lighting up with each line. "Today was tough," he would write, "but knowing you're waiting for me gives me strength. I saw a wildflower today, and it reminded me of the ones we picked up by the river last spring." These small details, seemingly insignificant, were threads weaving their love story, even from afar.

His sweetheart, back home, clung to these letters like precious treasures. She would read them by the fireplace, the flickering flames mirroring the emotions in her heart. In her replies, she poured out her own fears and hopes. "My love," she wrote, "I received your letter today, and it brought tears to my eyes. I wear your locket every day, and it feels like you are here with me. The town is quiet without you, but I find solace in our memories and dreams of our future." These exchanges became a ritual to keep their connection alive despite the distance and the unknown.

The impact of these letters extended beyond their immediate relationship. Their children and grandchildren would later read these letters, finding inspiration in the resilience and love captured in each word. "Your grandfather was a brave man," she would say, her voice tinged with pride and nostalgia, "and these letters were our lifeline." The letters taught their descendants the value of written communication, a tangible reminder of the power of words to bridge gaps and sustain love.

Years later, the war ended, and the young soldier returned home. Their reunion was filled with tears of joy and relief, the culmination of years of longing and hope. They married in a small, intimate ceremony, and their love letters became family heirlooms preserved in a wooden box. Whenever they faced challenges, they would read those letters, drawing strength from the love and resilience they had nurtured during the war.

These letters were more than just correspondence; they symbolized their unwavering love and commitment. They inspired future generations to value the art of letter writing, to pour their hearts into words, and to cherish the connections they build. Through these letters, their love story lived on, a testament to the enduring power of love in the face of adversity.

1.3 THE FAMILY QUILT

The family quilt is more than just a patchwork of fabric; it is a symbol of heritage and love, a tangible representation of our shared history. Each piece of fabric has its own story, its own significance. My grandmother, a masterful quilter, began this tradition. She collected pieces of fabric from various moments in our family's life, each patch carefully chosen for its meaning. A scrap from an old dress, a piece of a worn-out shirt, a fragment from a baby blanket. Every patch represented a different family member or milestone, making the quilt a living tapestry of our collective experiences.

The creation of the family quilt was a collaborative effort, a labor of love that brought us all together. Family members contributed their own pieces of fabric, each one adding a new layer to the quilt's story. During family gatherings, they would sit in a circle, stitching and chatting, sharing stories and laughter. It was a bonding experience, a way to connect with each other and the past.

Each patch in the quilt holds a memory, a story embedded in its threads. One patch was made from a piece of my grandmother's wedding dress, and its delicate lace is a reminder of the day she married my grandfather. Another patch comes from my father's childhood blanket; its soft, worn fabric is a testament to years of comfort and security. There is a patch commemorating a family reunion, its vibrant colors capturing the joy and excitement of that special day. Every piece of fabric is a fragment of our history, a piece of the puzzle that makes up our family's story.

The quilt's role in our family's ongoing story is profound. It is passed down from generation to generation, each new owner adding their own patches and memories. It has become a part of our family traditions, used in ceremonies and celebrations, a symbol of continuity and connection. A piece of their first blanket is added to the quilt when a new child is born. When a family member marries, a piece of their wedding attire is stitched into the fabric. The quilt grows with us, evolving as our family does. It is always a step behind us but never far.

The emotional value of the quilt cannot be overstated. It is a source of comfort and a reminder of where we come from. It is a link to our past, a way to connect with loved ones who are no longer with us. When we wrap ourselves in the quilt, we are enveloped in the warmth and love of our family. It is a reminder that we are part of something bigger than ourselves, a chain of generations linked by love and shared experiences. The quilt is more than just a fabric collection; it is a family heirloom, a treasure that holds our memories and love stitched together with care and devotion.

1.4 SIBLING SHENANIGANS

Siblings have a unique way of bringing both chaos and camaraderie into our lives. Growing up, my brother and I were best friends and the fiercest of rivals. One summer, we decided to build a secret treehouse in the giant oak tree behind our house. We gathered scrap wood and old nails, sneaking tools from Dad's garage. Our treehouse became a fortress of imagination, a place where we were pirates one day and astronauts the next. The thrill of working together, hiding from our parents, and creating something uniquely ours was exhilarating. It wasn't just a wooden structure but a symbol of our shared childhood and our adventures.

Of course, sibling relationships aren't all about cooperation. We were delighted to play pranks on each other and our parents. I remember the time we managed to convince our younger sister that the attic was haunted, complete with eerie sounds and flickering lights. The laughter we shared as she tiptoed around the house, wary of ghosts, was infectious. These playful moments, filled with mischief and creativity, forged a bond that has lasted a lifetime. They taught us to find joy in the small, everyday moments and cherish the laughter from just being together.

But beyond the pranks and playful antics, a deep bond and camaraderie forms between siblings. We supported each other through school challenges, whether it was helping with homework, studying for exams, or offering a shoulder to cry on after a tough day. We collaborated on household chores, turning mundane tasks into opportunities for teamwork. Washing dishes became a game, and mowing the lawn was a chance to chat and share dreams. These shared experiences created a foundation of trust and friendship that has stood the test of time.

Siblings also teach us invaluable life lessons. We learned the importance of sharing and compromise through countless arguments and reconciliations. When one of us wanted to watch cartoons and the other preferred a different show, we had to find a middle ground. These small negotiations in childhood prepared us for the more significant compromises required in adult relationships. Sibling rivalry also honed our problem-solving skills. Competing for the last cookie or the front seat in the car forced us to think creatively and find fair solutions. Though seemingly trivial, these interactions played a crucial role in our personal growth and development.

One of the most profound aspects of sibling relationships is the emotional support we provide each other. I remember the night my sister came home heartbroken after her first breakup. I didn't have all the answers, but just being there, listening, and offering comfort made a difference. Celebrating each other's successes is equally important. When my brother graduated from college, we threw a surprise party with homemade banners and his favorite cake. The joy and pride we felt were palpable, a testament to the strength of our bond.

In these ways, siblings become our confidants and companions, the people who understand us in ways no one else can. They know our secrets, our fears, and our dreams. They have seen us at our best and our worst and love us all the same. The playful and mischievous nature of sibling relationships, the deep bond and camaraderie, the lessons learned, and the emotional support provided all contribute to a unique and enduring connection. These relationships shape us, teach us, and give a sense of belonging that lasts a lifetime.

1.5 DAD'S FISHING LESSONS

Early mornings with Dad were a special kind of magic. We'd rise before dawn, the house still cloaked in darkness, and quietly gather our fishing gear. The drive to the lake was filled with a sense of adventure, the sky gradually lightening as the sun began its ascent. By the time we reached the water, rays of sunlight danced on the surface, casting a golden glow that promised a perfect day. The world seemed to hold its breath, the only sounds being the gentle lapping of the water and the occasional call of a bird. The serenity of those moments, the stillness broken only by our whispered conversations, created a sense of peace that I cherish to this day.

Fishing with Dad wasn't just about catching fish; it was about learning lessons that would stay with me for life. Patience was perhaps the most important. Sitting quietly, waiting for a fish to bite, taught me to appreciate the value of stillness and perseverance. Dad would often say, "Good things come to those who wait," and in those long, silent moments, I understood what he meant. The anticipation of the first catch was thrilling, but the waiting made it all the more rewarding when a fish finally took the bait. Respecting nature was another critical lesson. Dad always emphasized the importance of leaving no trace and appreciating the environment without harming it. We'd pick up any litter we found and make sure to release any fish that were too small. These principles of patience and respect extended beyond our fishing trips, shaping my approach to life and the world around me.

One particular trip stands out in my memory, a day when everything seemed to align perfectly. We'd been fishing for hours with little success when, suddenly, I felt a strong tug on my line. My heart raced as I struggled to reel in what felt like a giant. With Dad's guidance and encouragement, I finally managed to pull the fish out of the water. It was a massive bass, the biggest catch I'd ever seen. We both laughed and cheered, the excitement of the moment becoming a family legend we'd recount for years to come. Another time, I nearly caught a fish, but it slipped off the hook at the last second. I was devastated, but Dad comforted me, saying, "Sometimes, the ones that get away teach us more than the ones we catch." It was a lesson in handling disappointment and finding meaning in every experience.

Fishing trips also provided moments of deep connection and support. I remember a time when I was struggling with a personal issue, feeling lost and unsure. Dad sensed my turmoil and took me fishing, knowing the tranquility of the lake would help. As we sat there, lines cast, he offered gentle words of wisdom, sharing his own struggles and how he overcame them. His support and understanding gave me the strength to face my challenges, reinforcing the bond between us. These moments of comfort and guidance were invaluable, shaping my resilience and outlook on life.

In these ways, fishing with Dad was more than a pastime; it was a foundation for lifelong values and relationships. The lessons learned on those early morning trips to the lake have shaped who I am and how I approach the world. They are memories etched in my heart, threads woven into the fabric of my life.

2

HISTORICAL REFLECTIONS

When I was a child, history seemed like a distant, unchanging thing. My parents' and grandparents' tales of the Great Depression or World War II felt like stories from another world. But then came the moon landing in 1969, and suddenly, history was right there, unfolding before our eyes. That summer, my family and I crowded into our living room, the black-and-white television flickering with images that would become iconic. It was an event that brought the world together, and for the first time, I felt like we were part of something much bigger.

2.1 THE MOON LANDING WATCH PARTY

The days leading up to July 20, 1969, were filled with anticipation. It seemed like the whole world was buzzing with excitement. Families gathered around their black-and-white televisions, neighborhood watch parties sprang up, and there was a palpable sense of national pride. My family was no different. We invited friends and neighbors over, and the living room transformed into a mini-theater. The television, usually reserved for evening news, became the focal point of our gathering. Snacks and drinks were laid out, and everyone took their seats, eager to witness history in the making.

As the countdown began, the room was filled with a mix of excitement and nervous energy. The adults marveled at the technological advancements that had made this moment possible, while the kids, myself included, asked endless questions about space and astronauts. "How do they breathe up there?" "What if they float away?" My father, a man who had lived through the war and seen the dawn of the automobile and the airplane, shared his memories of earlier space missions. He talked about the awe he felt when Sputnik was launched and how he never imagined humans would walk on the moon in his lifetime.

The room erupted in cheers when the Eagle lunar module finally touched down. But it was the moment when Neil Armstrong stepped onto the moon and uttered those famous words, "That's one small step for man, one giant leap for mankind," that the room fell into a peaceful silence. The gravity of the moment was not lost on anyone. We sat there, eyes glued to the screen, as Armstrong and Buzz Aldrin explored the lunar surface. It felt surreal, almost like a dream, but the images on the screen were a testament to human ingenuity and perseverance.

The conversations that followed were filled with awe and wonder. The adults discussed the future of space exploration, speculating about Mars and beyond. Inspired by what they had seen, the children began to dream of becoming astronauts. With a twinkle in his eye, my father recalled how he once dreamed of flying but never had the chance (until that moment. He did later). He looked at us and said, "You kids will see things we never even imagined. The sky isn't the limit anymore."

The moon landing was more than just a technological achievement; it was a unifying event. It brought people together in shared wonder and pride, if only for a moment. The sense of accomplishment was palpable, not just in our living room, but across the USA and the world. It was a reminder of what we could achieve when we worked together toward a common goal. For us children, it was a glimpse of the future, a spark that ignited our imaginations and expanded our horizons.

Years later, the moon landing watch party remains a cherished family memory. The sense of unity and accomplishment we felt that day stayed with us, inspiring dreams and aspirations. It was a moment when history came alive, not just on the television screen, but in our hearts and minds. The lessons of that day—the importance of curiosity, perseverance, and unity—continue to resonate, reminding us of the extraordinary potential within us all.

2.2 THE SUMMER OF WOODSTOCK

The summer of 1969 was electric. The air buzzed with the spirit of change, fueled by the counterculture movement that challenged societal norms and embraced peace, love, and freedom ideals. Thousands of young people gathered in Bethel, New York, drawn by the promise of music and unity. They came from all corners, hitchhiking, piling into car caravans, and walking miles to reach the festival grounds. This was Woodstock, a celebration of music and a symbol of a generation's desire for a better world. Iconic performers like Jimi Hendrix, Janis Joplin, and The Who were set to take the stage, promising an unforgettable experience.

The journey to Woodstock was an adventure in itself. Imagine the scene—roads clogged with cars, each packed with eager festival-goers. People leaned out of windows, sharing stories and laughter, the anticipation palpable. Some had to abandon their vehicles and walk, backpacks slung over their shoulders, but no one seemed to mind. The excitement and camaraderie among the crowd made the miles melt away. Along the way, strangers became friends, united by the shared goal of reaching this historic gathering.

Upon arriving, the atmosphere was unlike anything ever experienced. Despite the rain that turned fields into muddy swamps and the makeshift tents that offered little protection, the sense of peace and community prevailed. Food and supplies were shared generously, and strangers helped each other without hesitation. It was as if, for those few days, the world outside ceased to exist, replaced by a utopia where kindness and solidarity reigned supreme. The music added to this magic, with performances that would go down in history. Joplin's soulful voice echoed through the fields, touching hearts and lifting spirits.

There were many challenges, but they only added to the event's spirit. The muddy fields became a playground for impromptu mudslides, laughter ringing out as people embraced the mess. Makeshift shelters were erected, and people huddled together for warmth, sharing stories and songs late into the night. The lack of proper facilities and food shortages could have dampened spirits, but instead, it fostered a sense of resilience and resourcefulness. The collective feeling of being part of something historic, something bigger than themselves, buoyed everyone. It was a time of pure, unfiltered connection, where the barriers of everyday life melted away.

Woodstock's cultural impact was profound and lasting. It wasn't just a music festival; it was a cultural phenomenon that encapsulated the ethos of an entire generation. The festival's influence on music and culture can still be felt today, a testament to its enduring legacy. Personal stories from those who attended reveal the transformative power of those days. Many speak of how the experience broadened their horizons, instilling in them a lifelong belief in the power of community and the importance of standing up for one's ideals. The message of peace, love, and music continues to resonate, a reminder of what can be achieved when people come together with open hearts and minds.

The memories of Woodstock are etched in the minds of those who were there, cherished, and recounted with a sparkle in their eyes. The festival changed lives, inspiring new paths and new ways of thinking. It wasn't just about the music; it was about the connections, lessons learned, and the realization that change was possible. Woodstock's legacy lives on, as a beacon of hope and a symbol of a time when anything seemed possible.

2.3 THE MAGIC OF RADIO

Radio was once the heartbeat of the home, a source of entertainment and information that brought families together. In the evenings, after dinner, families would gather around the radio, the soft glow of the dial casting a warm light in the room. It was a ritual where everyone would sit close, hanging on to every word and sound from the speakers—the latest hits played during morning routines, setting the tone for the day ahead. The radio was more than a device; it was a companion, a storyteller that connected people to the wider world.

Popular radio programs captured the imagination of listeners in ways that television could never replicate. Suspenseful dramas like "The Shadow" kept everyone on the edge of their seats, the eerie voice of the narrator sending shivers down spines. Comedy programs, such as "Amos 'n' Andy," brought laughter into homes, offering a much-needed escape from the daily grind. These shows became part of the fabric of daily life, their characters and catchphrases weaving their way into everyday conversations. The radio transported listeners to different worlds, whether it was the bustling streets of a detective story or the cozy kitchen of a comedy.

Radio DJs and personalities became beloved figures, their voices as familiar as those of family members. A DJ's signature sign-off phrase could become a household saying, repeated with a smile each time the radio was turned off. Listeners would call in to request songs, dedicate tunes to loved ones, and share their stories. These interactions created a sense of community, a feeling that, despite the physical distance, people were connected through the airwaves. DJs were influencers long before the term existed, shaping musical tastes and cultural conversations with their choices and commentary.

The communal experience of radio was something special. Neighbors would chat over the fence about last night's episode, dissecting plot twists and character developments. Kids would imitate radio characters during playtime, their imaginations fueled by the stories they heard. It was a shared enjoyment that transcended individual households, creating bonds and sparking friendships. The radio was a common thread that connected communities, a source of shared joy and collective experience.

Radio was also a lifeline during times of crisis. During World War II, families would huddle around the radio, listening intently to news broadcasts and updates from the front lines. President Franklin D. Roosevelt's "fireside chats" offered comfort and reassurance, his calm voice a beacon of hope in uncertain times. Major news events, like the Lindbergh baby kidnapping or the Hindenburg disaster, were first heard through the radio, the immediacy of the medium bringing the world into living rooms in real-time.

The radio's role in shaping cultural and social norms cannot be overstated. It was the medium through which new music genres were introduced, from the big bands of the '30s and '40s to the rock and roll revolution of the '50s and '60s. It provided a platform for diverse voices and perspectives, broadening listeners' horizons and fostering a sense of inclusivity. Radio was a teacher, an entertainer, and a friend, its influence felt in countless ways.

The golden age of radio may have passed, but its legacy endures. The magic of those moments, the shared experiences, and the connections forged through the airwaves remain vivid in the memories of those who lived through it. Radio was more than just a way to pass the time; it was a vital part of daily life, a source of comfort, joy, and community. The stories it told and the voices it amplified continue to resonate, a testament to the enduring power of this humble yet transformative medium.

2.4 SCHOOL DAYS AND FIRST CRUSHES

The start of a new school year always brought a mix of excitement and nerves. You remember that first day, clutching a fresh notebook and a sharpened pencil, feeling a sense of possibility. The smell of new textbooks and the sound of lockers clanging shut were the soundtrack to those years. The classroom was a world of its own, where each desk held a story. Participating in school plays and talent shows added layers to those memories. You'd rehearse lines or practice dance moves, your heart pounding with both fear and anticipation on opening night. The applause from the audience, especially if your parents were there, made all the nervousness worth it.

Friendships formed in those school hallways were unlike any other. Best friends passed notes during class, each folded message a secret treasure. Lunchtime gatherings were a daily ritual, where you shared everything from sandwiches to secrets. Recess adventures turned the playground into a kingdom, with games that felt as grand as any epic tale. Those friendships were the foundation of your social life, the bonds that made school not just bearable but enjoyable. You navigated the complexities of growing up together, each friendship a lifeline in the ever-changing landscape of adolescence.

First crushes added an innocent charm to those school days. Do you recall the butterflies in your stomach as you nervously wrote a Valentine's Day card for your crush? The way your heart raced when you saw them in the hallway, and the blush that crept to your cheeks when you accidentally made eye contact. With its awkwardness and innocence, young love was a rite of passage.

Each crush was a lesson in bravery, teaching you to put yourself out there and risk the vulnerability that comes with caring for someone. Those emotions, raw and unfiltered, were both exhilarating and terrifying.

Favorite teachers left an indelible mark on your heart. There was always that one teacher who saw something special in you, who encouraged you to reach for the stars. Perhaps a teacher fostered your passion for reading, introducing you to books that opened up new worlds. Or it was the one who made math or science come alive, turning complex concepts into understandable ideas. Celebrating a teacher's birthday with a surprise party was a way to give back a fraction of the joy they brought into your life. Their influence went beyond the classroom, shaping your interests and aspirations in ways you still carry.

School life was a tapestry of routines and memorable moments. The excitement of a new school year, the friendships that felt like lifelines, the innocent charm of first crushes, and the lasting impact of supportive educators all combined to create a rich, multifaceted experience. Each day brought new challenges and joys, shaping you into the person you are today. The lessons learned and the memories are also reminders of the journey you've traveled.

2.5 MEMORIES OF THE BERLIN WALL FALLING

The Berlin Wall stood as a stark symbol of division for nearly three decades. Erected in 1961, it split Berlin into East and West, a physical manifestation of the Cold War tensions that gripped the world. Families, friends, and lovers found themselves on opposite sides, their lives torn apart by concrete and barbed wire. The Wall became a grim reminder of the ideological chasm between the communist East and the capitalist West, a barrier fortified by guards, dogs, and watchtowers. For many, it represented the loss of freedom and the harsh reality of living under constant surveillance.

On the night of November 9, 1989, the atmosphere in Berlin was electric. Word had spread that the East German government was easing travel restrictions, and people flocked to the Wall, driven by a mixture of excitement and disbelief. The air buzzed with anticipation as crowds gathered, their faces illuminated by streetlights and the glow of camera flashes. Families who had been separated for years reunited at the Brandenburg Gate, their tearful embraces a poignant testament to the human cost of the Wall. The sounds of chisels and hammers breaking through the concrete filled the air, a cacophony of liberation.

Among the crowd was a family that had been divided since the Wall's construction. They met at the Brandenburg Gate, tears streaming down their faces as they hugged tightly, refusing to let go. Nearby, young people from East and West Berlin introduced themselves to each other, their laughter and animated conversations a stark contrast to the years of silence and separation. Emotional speeches echoed through the night, capturing the collective joy and relief of a city finally coming together. The celebrations continued into the early hours, with people singing, dancing, and toasting their newfound freedom.

The fall of the Berlin Wall had a profound impact on individuals and the world at large. For the people of Berlin, it marked the beginning of a new era filled with hope and the promise of unity. The sense of freedom was palpable, as restrictions lifted and opportunities opened up. Yet, the reunification of Germany came with its own set of challenges. Integrating two distinct societies, each with its own economic and social systems, was no small feat.

There were obstacles to overcome, but the spirit of unity and determination prevailed.

Globally, the fall of the Wall symbolized the end of the Cold War, a turning point in modern history. It heralded the collapse of communist regimes across Eastern Europe and the spread of democratic ideals. The images of Berliners tearing down the Wall with their bare hands became iconic, a powerful representation of the human spirit's resilience and the universal longing for freedom. The event inspired movements for change around the world, proving that even the most formidable barriers could be dismantled.

The memories of that night remain vivid for those who lived through it. The joy, the tears, the sense of possibility—all these emotions are etched in the hearts of Berliners. The fall of the Wall was more than just a political event; it was a deeply personal experience that touched the lives of millions. It reminded us of the importance of unity, the strength of the human spirit, and the enduring power of hope. The legacy of that night continues to inspire, a beacon of what can be achieved when people come together to fight for their freedoms.

In closing, the fall of the Berlin Wall was a monumental event that reshaped the world and left an indelible mark on the hearts of those who witnessed it. As we move forward in this book, let us carry the lessons of unity, resilience, and hope, exploring more stories that remind us of the extraordinary moments that define our shared history.

3

NATURE AND THE OUTDOORS

Those who have been there remember the first time they set foot in Yosemite National Park. Your senses are overwhelmed by the sheer majesty of the landscape. The towering sequoias reach skyward, their ancient trunks standing as silent witnesses to centuries gone by. Each tree seems to tell a story, its bark etched with the passage of time. The air crisp and filled with the scent of pine. Walking among these giants, you feel a sense of awe and humility. It is like nature reminding you of your small place in the grand tapestry of life.

3.1 THE BEAUTY OF NATIONAL PARKS

National parks are treasures of natural beauty and diversity. Regardless of the country it is in, each National Park offers a unique glimpse into the splendor of the natural world. Kruger in South Africa. Banff in Canada. Or Yosemite, in the USA. Its famed waterfalls cascade down granite cliffs, creating a symphony of water that can be heard from miles away. The park's granite rock formations, like El Capitan and Half Dome, are marvels of nature, sculpted over millennia by the forces of wind and water. Walking through Yosemite, you can't help but feel connected to something timeless and grand.

Then there's Yellowstone National Park, where the earth seems alive. The geysers and hot springs are like windows into the planet's fiery heart. With its predictable eruptions, Old Faithful never fails to draw a crowd. But beyond the famous geyser, Yellowstone is home to a rich tapestry of wildlife. Bison roam the plains, and if you're lucky, you might even spot a grizzly bear or a majestic bald eagle soaring overhead. The park's diverse ecosystems, from lush forests to geothermal wonders, make it a place of endless discovery for young and old.

The Grand Tetons, with their rugged beauty, offer a different kind of wilderness experience. The sharp, jagged peaks rise dramatically from the valley floor, creating a stunning backdrop for outdoor adventures. Here, you can hike over 250 miles of trails, each offering breathtaking views of the mountains and the pristine lakes that dot the landscape. Wildlife abounds, and it's not uncommon to see moose grazing in the meadows or hear the call of a distant elk. The Grand Tetons are a testament to nature's raw, untamed beauty.

Visiting these parks isn't just about seeing the sights; it's about experiencing the natural world in all its glory. Wildlife watching is a popular activity, and there's nothing quite like the thrill of spotting a bear or an eagle in its natural habitat. Hiking trails offer a chance to immerse yourself in the landscape, each step revealing new wonders. And for those who love the night sky, camping under a blanket of stars is an experience like no other. The Milky Way stretches across the sky, and the peaceful stillness of the night is a balm for the soul.

The restorative power of nature is one of its greatest gifts. Time spent in the great outdoors can rejuvenate the mind and body. The sound of a babbling brook or the rustling of leaves in the wind can soothe even the most troubled spirit. Early mornings in the parks, when the mist hangs low over the lakes and the world is still waking up, offer moments of profound peace. It's in these quiet times that you can truly connect with the natural world and find a sense of tranquility that's hard to come by in our busy lives.

National parks are more than just destinations; I feel they are sanctuaries for the soul. Each visit is a reminder of the beauty and wonder of the natural world, a chance to reconnect with the earth and with ourselves. Whether you're hiking a trail, watching wildlife, or simply sitting quietly by a lake, the parks offer moments of reflection and joy. So pack a bag, lace up your hiking boots, and set out to explore the grandeur of these national treasures. You'll find that nature speaks to you and reminds you of the simple pleasures and profound wonders that life has to offer.

3.2 STARGAZING NIGHTS

There's something magical about setting up for a night of stargazing. The anticipation builds as you gather blankets and telescopes, seeking out the perfect, quiet spot away from city lights. Laying out the blankets, you feel the cool grass beneath you, a stark contrast to the warmth of the day. As the sky darkens, the first stars appear, twinkling like tiny beacons in the vast expanse above. The excitement in the air is palpable, a mixture of awe and curiosity about the wonders that await in the night sky.

Identifying stars and constellations is an adventure in itself. With a star map or a handy app, you can locate familiar constellations like Orion, the Big Dipper, and Cassiopeia. My father always had a knack for this. He'd point out the constellations and tell us the myths and legends behind them. "That's Orion, the mighty hunter," he'd say, weaving tales of his adventures. The stories made the stars come alive, transforming the sky into a canvas of ancient lore. It wasn't just about finding stars; it was about connecting with the stories that have been told for generations.

One of the most memorable moments in stargazing is spotting a shooting star. The sudden streak of light across the sky catches everyone's breath. In that split second, you make a wish, a tradition that never loses its charm, no matter how old you get. Then, there's the thrill of finding a planet or a distant galaxy. With a good telescope, you might see the rings of Saturn or the moons of Jupiter, and each discovery is a little miracle. The shared silence and wonder while gazing at the stars create a bond that's hard to describe. It's as if, for that moment, time stands still, and the universe reveals its secrets.

These nights under the stars are more than just a pastime; they are a source of inspiration and curiosity. They remind us of the vastness of the universe and our small place within it. The memories created on these nights are as enduring as the stars themselves. Gazing up, you feel a connection to everyone who has ever looked at the same sky, a thread that links us across time and space. These moments foster a sense of wonder that stays with you, sparking questions and dreams that can last a lifetime, especially when you realize that we and everything around us are all made of the same stuff as the stars.

Stargazing has become a cherished family tradition for many. It's not just about looking at stars; it's about the time spent together, the stories shared, and the memories made. Whether it's a special occasion or just a clear night, these stargazing sessions bring people closer. They offer a break from the routine, a chance to reconnect with nature and each other. As you lay there, wrapped in blankets, the world falls away, leaving only the stars and the sense of peace they bring.

The tradition of stargazing can be passed down through generations. Each new stargazer adds their own stories and memories to the mix, creating a rich tapestry of shared experiences. Children learn from their parents and grandparents and, in turn, teach their own kids, keeping the tradition alive. I spent many hours reading astronomy books throughout the years as a result of nights of stargazing.

In the quiet moments of stargazing, you find a sense of belonging. The stars above, constant and unchanging, provide a comforting presence. They remind us that no matter where we are or what we're going through, the same sky stretches above us all.

3.3 A WALK IN THE AUTUMN WOODS

Imagine stepping into an autumn forest, the vibrant colors of the changing leaves painting a picture that seems almost too beautiful to be real. The reds, oranges, and yellows blend together in a breathtaking mosaic, each leaf a tiny masterpiece. The crisp, cool air fills your lungs with an invigorating freshness, while the smell of fallen leaves brings a sense of nostalgia and comfort. As you walk, the crunch of leaves underfoot creates a satisfying rhythm, each step a reminder of the season's beauty. It's a sensory experience that engages you fully, drawing you into the heart of nature's autumnal splendor.

Walking through the woods, you might spot wildlife preparing for the winter months ahead. A squirrel scurries up a tree, its cheeks puffed out with acorns. Birds flit from branch to branch, their songs a cheerful accompaniment to your stroll. Occasionally, you might find hidden treasures like brightly colored leaves or a perfectly formed acorn, nature's little gifts scattered along the path. The peacefulness and solitude of the forest envelop you, providing a sanctuary away from the hustle and bustle of daily life. It's a place where you can lose yourself in the moment, letting the worries of the world drift away with the falling leaves.

Conversations often take on a deeper, more meaningful tone during these walks. The natural setting seems to invite reflection and sharing. I recall many walks with my parents, where they would share stories from their youth. These tales of simpler times, adventures, and lessons learned were like a window into the past. As we walked, the forest around us seemed to listen, the rustling leaves and whispering wind adding a sense of intimacy to our conversations. These moments of quiet reflection and appreciation, surrounded by nature's beauty, created a profound and enduring bond.

The impact of these autumn walks on well-being and family bonds is undeniable. They became a cherished family tradition, a way to connect with each other and with nature. I know many families have this exact same tradition, as nature forms such a perfect background for bringing people together. The mental and emotional benefits of spending time in the forest are well-documented, from reducing stress to improving mood and overall health. There's something inherently calming about being surrounded by trees, the rhythm of walking, and the sights and sounds of the forest. It's an experience that brings a sense of peace and rejuvenation, a reminder of the simple pleasures in life.

These walks also inspire a deeper appreciation for the outdoors. Each visit to the forest reveals something new, whether it's a different species of bird, a unique leaf pattern, or the changing landscape as the seasons progress. It's a reminder of the ever-evolving beauty of nature and the importance of preserving it for future generations. The inspiration to continue exploring and appreciating the outdoors becomes a part of who you are, a lifelong love affair with nature that enriches your life in countless ways.

There's a particular walk that stands out in my memory. It was a golden afternoon, the sun casting long shadows through the trees. My mother, my brother, and I were walking along a familiar path, one we had taken many times before since we were kids. She stopped to pick up a particularly beautiful leaf, its colors vivid against the forest floor. "Isn't it amazing," she said, holding the leaf up to the light, "how something so simple can be so beautiful?" It was a small moment that captured the essence of our walks: finding beauty in the small things, sharing quiet moments of connection, and creating memories that would last.

3.4 SEASIDE RETREATS

The seaside has always held a special place in my heart. There's something undeniably calming about the rhythmic sound of waves crashing on the shore. It's as if the ocean itself is breathing, creating a soothing melody that washes away stress and worry. The salty sea air invigorates your senses, filling your lungs with a freshness that's hard to find elsewhere. The feel of warm sand between your toes is a simple yet profound pleasure. Warmed by the sun, each grain seems to carry a bit of the sea's magic. Walking along the beach, you feel a connection to the earth and the endless horizon stretching before you.

Growing up, we lived inland, but I have had the luxury of living by the sea for the last ten years. I can't imagine being without my daily beach walks.

Beach visits offer a treasure trove of activities that bring joy and relaxation. Building sandcastles with children or grandchildren is a timeless pastime. The creativity involved in molding towers and moats, only to see them gently washed away by the tide, is a lesson in impermanence and joy. Collecting seashells adds another layer of enjoyment. Each shell, unique in its shape and color, becomes a keepsake of your time by the sea. Swimming in the ocean and feeling the cool water against your skin is refreshing and exhilarating. For the more adventurous, surfing the waves offers a rush like no other, a dance with the sea that challenges and thrills.

The beauty of coastal landscapes is unparalleled. Dramatic cliffs rise majestically from the shore, their rugged faces carved by the relentless force of the ocean. Hidden coves, accessible only by foot or boat, offer secluded spots of paradise where you can escape the world. Tide pools, teeming with marine life, are like miniature ecosystems waiting to be explored. Peering into these pools, you might see tiny crabs scuttling about or colorful sea anemones swaying with the current. Each visit to the coast reveals new wonders, a reminder of the ocean's vast and varied beauty.

One of my fondest memories is of our family's annual beach getaway when we were kids. Every summer, we'd pack up the car and head to the coast, eager for a week of sun, sand, and sea. The days were filled with laughter and adventure, whether we were building elaborate sandcastles, flying kites, or simply lounging under beach umbrellas. Evenings were magical, with bonfires on the sand, roasting marshmallows, and sharing stories under a canopy of stars. These trips were more than just vacations; they were a time for family bonding and creating memories that we cherished year after year.

Another memory that stands out is a seaside picnic with some good friends years later. We found a secluded spot on the beach, laid out a blanket, and enjoyed a simple meal of fresh fruit, cheese, and wine as the sun set over the horizon. The sky was painted in hues of pink and orange, and the gentle sound of the waves created the perfect backdrop for our quiet conversation. As the sun dipped below the horizon, we watched the first stars appear and felt grateful for the moment. It was a perfect evening, a reminder of the beauty of simplicity, friendship, and the magic of the seaside.

The seaside, with its calming atmosphere and endless beauty, offers a sanctuary where you can reconnect with nature and yourself. Whether you're busy with activities or simply sitting quietly and watching the waves, each moment by the sea is a gift. The memories created during these visits are treasures that stay with you, bringing joy and peace long after you've left the shore.

3.5 THE SECRET FISHING SPOT

Discovering our secret fishing spot felt like stepping into a hidden world. The journey started with a trek through a dense forest, the path barely visible beneath layers of fallen leaves. Each step brought a sense of adventure, the thrill of finding a place known only to close family members. We had to navigate through a maze of trees, cross a small creek, and climb over moss-covered rocks. But the moment we arrived, all the effort felt worthwhile. The secluded spot by the river was our sanctuary, a place untouched by the outside world. The shared secret strengthened our family bonds, creating a special connection that only we understood.

Fishing there was more than a hobby; it was a cherished tradition. We'd cast our lines, the gentle plop of the bait hitting the water breaking the serene silence. Patience was key, waiting for that telltale tug on the line. The types of fish we caught varied with the seasons. We'd reel in trout in spring, their silvery scales glistening in the sunlight. Summer brought bass, their fights making each catch a thrilling challenge. Techniques passed down from generation to generation made each trip a learning experience. Dad taught us the art of reeling in a catch without losing it. These lessons were more than just practical skills; they were pieces of wisdom that connected us to our heritage.

One particularly bountiful day stands out in my memory. The river seemed alive with fish, each cast yielding a catch. We filled our baskets quickly, each fish adding to the sense of triumph. The camaraderie during these trips was palpable. We'd share stories, laugh at old jokes, and enjoy the simple pleasure of each other's company. On another occasion, I nearly caught the biggest fish I'd ever seen. It was a battle of wills, the fish pulling with all its might. Just as I thought I had it, the line snapped, and the fish swam away, leaving me with a mix of frustration and amusement. We laughed about it for years, the tale of the one that got away becoming a family legend.

The secret fishing spot became a refuge, a place where we could escape the stresses of daily life when we grew older. The tranquility of the river, the sound of water flowing over rocks, and the rustle of leaves in the wind created a sense of peace. It was a place where time seemed to slow down, allowing us to relax and reconnect with nature and each other. The tradition of visiting the spot has been maintained over the years, with each trip adding new layers to our shared history. It's more than just a location; it's a symbol of family unity, a place where memories are made and cherished.In this secret haven, the world's worries melt away. The simple act of fishing and of being together in nature brings a sense of fulfillment that's hard to find elsewhere. The spot holds a special place in our hearts.

As we wrap up our exploration of nature and the outdoors, let's carry forward the simple lessons and profound joys these experiences bring. From the grandeur of national parks to the intimate moments by a secret fishing spot, nature offers us a chance to reconnect with ourselves and our loved ones.

Now, let's turn our focus to another cherished aspect of life: the stories of love and gratitude that enrich our days.

4

LOVE AND GRATITUDE

One of my favorite memories involves an old couple I met while volunteering at a community event. They were celebrating their 50th wedding anniversary, and their love was palpable. They moved in perfect harmony, finishing each other's sentences and sharing knowing glances. It was clear that their bond had only grown stronger with time, weathering the ups and downs of life. Watching them, I realized that nurtured love becomes a powerful force that can withstand time.

4.1 A LOVE THAT LASTS

Enduring love is a testament to the strength and beauty of long-term relationships. Imagine a couple celebrating their golden anniversary—fifty years of shared life, filled with countless moments that have defined their journey together. The daily routines, often taken for granted, become the threads that weave their bond even tighter. Simple acts like making morning coffee or taking an evening walk hand in hand keep their connection strong. These small, everyday gestures are the glue that holds their relationship together, reminding them of their commitment and affection.

Traveling together creates shared adventures that enrich their relationship. Each trip, whether a grand tour of Europe or a weekend getaway to a nearby town, adds a new chapter to their story. They explore new places, try new foods, and experience different cultures while leaning on each other for support and companionship. These adventures bring them closer, offering opportunities to learn and grow together. Overcoming challenges, whether they are logistical hiccups during travel or more significant life obstacles, strengthens their bond. They navigate these hurdles side by side, emerging stronger and more united.

Every long-term relationship has its share of challenges, but how couples face them defines their enduring love. Whether dealing with health scares or financial difficulties, they support each other through thick and thin. Imagine the unwavering support of a partner during a health crisis. The comforting presence, the reassuring words, and the constant care make all the difference. Celebrating each other's achievements and milestones also plays a critical role. Whether it's a promotion at work, a personal accomplishment, or a special anniversary, taking the time to acknowledge and celebrate these moments reinforces their bond.

Small acts of love keep relationships alive and thriving. Holding hands during a walk in the park might seem insignificant, but it's a powerful gesture of connection and intimacy. It's a reminder of their shared journey and the comfort of knowing they are not alone. Preparing a favorite meal for each other is another simple act that speaks volumes. It shows thoughtfulness and a desire to bring joy to the other person's day. These everyday gestures, though small, have a profound impact, keeping the flame of love burning bright.

Unwavering support and companionship are the cornerstones of enduring love. Being there for each other during health scares, offering comfort and care, and celebrating each other's achievements and milestones solidify their bond. The little things, like a reassuring hug or a word of encouragement, make a big difference —knowing that they can rely on each other, no matter what, creates a sense of security and trust that is hard to break. This support system becomes their rock, the foundation for their relationship.

Long-term relationships are a beautiful testament to the power of love and commitment. They remind us that love, when nurtured and cherished, can stand the test of time. Daily routines, shared experiences, small acts of love, and unwavering support create an unbreakable bond.

As you reflect on your own relationships, may you find inspiration in these stories of enduring love, and may they remind you of the beauty and strength that come from a lifetime of shared moments and cherished memories.

Reflection Section: Reflecting on Enduring Love

Take a moment to think about the long-term relationships in your life. It doesn't necessarily be your spouse. What are the small acts of love that have kept those relationships strong? How have shared experiences and unwavering support impacted your journey together? Write down your thoughts and memories, and let them remind you of the enduring power of love.

4.2 ACTS OF KINDNESS

One of the most touching moments I witnessed was when a neighbor helped an elderly woman with her groceries. It was a simple act, yet the impact was profound. The woman's face lit up with gratitude, and you could see the relief in her eyes. It reminded me of the power of small, everyday kindnesses. These gestures, like holding the door for someone or offering a smile, can make a big difference in someone's day. They create a ripple effect, inspiring others to act kindly as well. Imagine receiving a handwritten note of encouragement. The effort behind such a gesture can lift your spirits and remind you that someone cares.

Kindness has a way of spreading. I remember when our community came together to support a family in need. It all started with a few neighbors organizing a bake sale to raise funds. Soon, others joined in, offering their time, resources, and skills. The result was a heartwarming display of unity and compassion.

Another example is a classroom project that encouraged students to perform acts of kindness. From helping classmates with homework to organizing a school-wide charity drive, the project created a culture of empathy and generosity. No matter how small, each act contributed to a larger wave of kindness that touched everyone involved.

Unexpected kindness from strangers can leave a lasting impression. One day, while at a coffee shop, I saw a stranger pay for someone's coffee. The recipient's surprise and gratitude were evident. It was a brief interaction, but it brightened both their days. Another instance was when a friend lost his wallet, and a stranger found it and returned it with everything intact. The relief and gratitude he felt were immense. These acts of kindness remind us of the goodness in people and restore our faith in humanity. They show that even in a world filled with challenges, kindness can break through and make a difference.

The personal fulfillment that comes from giving kindness is immeasurable. Volunteering at a local shelter, for instance, brings immense joy. Seeing the smiles and hearing the heartfelt thanks of those you help is incredibly rewarding. It's not just about the act itself but the connections you make and your positive impact. Donating time or resources to a cause close to your heart brings a sense of purpose and satisfaction.

Whether mentoring a young student, planting trees in a community park, or simply spending time with a lonely person, these acts enrich both the giver and the receiver.

Reflection Section: Acts of Kindness

Think about a time when you received or gave an act of kindness. How did it make you feel? What was the impact on you or the other person?

4.3 THANKSGIVING TRADITIONS

Thanksgiving has always been a time of warmth and togetherness. The kitchen becomes the bustling heart of the home, filled with the sound of clattering pots and the aroma of roasting turkey. Everyone has a role to play. Grandma might be rolling out the dough for her famous pumpkin pie while Dad carves the turkey with the precision of a surgeon. The younger ones set the table, carefully placing each piece of silverware and folding napkins into little shapes.

Preparing the Thanksgiving feast is a family affair, a symphony of coordinated chaos that brings everyone together. The laughter, the shared tasks, and the anticipation of the meal create a sense of unity that lingers long after the last dish is washed and put away.

Another cherished tradition is watching the Thanksgiving Day parade. Families gather in the living room, snuggled under blankets with hot cocoa in hand. The floats, the marching bands, and the giant balloons bring a sense of wonder and excitement. It's a time to relax and enjoy each other's company, sharing stories and reminiscing about Thanksgivings past. This simple act of coming together to watch the parade has become a ritual for millions of families looking forward to, a way to kick off the holiday festivities and set the tone for the day.

The expressions of gratitude shared around the Thanksgiving table are some of the most heartfelt moments of the holiday. As family members sit down to the feast, they take turns sharing what they are grateful for. The responses range from the profound to the simple, each one a glimpse into the hearts of our loved ones. "I'm grateful for my health," someone might say, while another adds, "I'm thankful for this family and the love we share." These moments of giving thanks remind us of the blessings in our lives and the importance of appreciating them. Some years, we write gratitude letters and read them aloud, each word a testament to our appreciation and love.

Thanksgiving is also a time for giving and helping others. Many families, including ours, make it a point to volunteer at a soup kitchen or organize a food drive for the local community. Serving a meal to those in need or collecting donations for a food bank brings a sense of fulfillment and purpose. It's a way to extend the spirit of Thanksgiving beyond our own table and into the community. These acts of giving and sharing reinforce the values of compassion and generosity, reminding us that the holiday is about more than just food and family—it's about making a positive impact on the lives of others.

Nostalgia plays a significant role in Thanksgiving celebrations. Grandma's famous pumpkin pie recipe passed down through generations, is a staple at our feast. The smell of the pie baking in the oven evokes memories of Thanksgivings past, of family members who are no longer with us but whose presence is felt in every bite. The annual family football game in the backyard is another tradition that brings joy and laughter. Young and old alike take to the field, the competitive spirit tempered by the sheer fun of the game. These nostalgic elements create a sense of continuity and connection, linking the past with the present and carrying our traditions forward.

Thanksgiving is a tapestry of warmth, gratitude, and togetherness. The preparation of the feast, the shared expressions of thanks, the acts of giving, and the nostalgic traditions all come together to create a holiday that is rich in meaning and joy. Each year, as we gather around the table and share a meal, we are reminded of the blessings in our lives and the importance of cherishing them. Thanksgiving is more than just a holiday; it is a celebration of love, family, and the enduring bonds that connect us all.

4.4 THE JOY OF GIVING

There's a unique thrill in choosing the perfect gift for a loved one. You wander through shops or browse online, picturing their face lighting up when they see what you've picked just for them. It's not about the cost or grandeur but the thought and care behind the choice. The sparkle in their eyes, the genuine smile, and the heartfelt thank you make every moment of searching worthwhile. You might, for instance, remember that time you found the perfect scarf for your sister—a color that matched her eyes and a softness that reminded her of your shared childhood. The joy of giving transcends the material, creating a bond that's felt deeply and remembered fondly.

Acts of selfless giving often create profound impacts. I remember when I donated to a charity that helps needy children. The knowledge that my contribution could provide a child with books, meals, or a safe place to sleep was immensely rewarding. The letters of thanks from the organization, with photos of smiling children, made it all real. It's incredible how a single act of generosity can ripple out, touching lives in ways you might never fully grasp.

Another memorable instance was when our community came together to build a playground. Everyone pitched in—some brought tools, others provided snacks, and many offered their time and labor. The finished playground wasn't just a space for kids to play; it was a testament to community spirit and collective effort, a gift from many hearts to the next generation.

Giving comes in many forms, not all wrapped in paper with bows. Sometimes, the most valuable gift you can offer is your time.

Spending a day with someone who's lonely can make a world of difference. I recall visiting a neighbor who lived alone. We spent hours chatting, drinking tea, and reminiscing. Her gratitude was immense, and I left feeling enriched by the experience.

Sharing your skills and knowledge is another meaningful way to give. Whether teaching a grandchild to bake, helping a friend with a tech issue, or mentoring someone at work, sharing builds connections and fosters growth.

The long-term impact of giving can be transformative. Consider a scholarship fund that helps students achieve their dreams. Each recipient, empowered by education, contributes to society in meaningful ways. It's a gift that keeps on giving, creating a legacy of opportunity and success. Mentorship programs offer similar benefits. Guiding young people towards their goals, offering advice, and sharing experiences can positively shape their futures. The ripple effect of these acts of giving is profound, touching not just individuals but entire communities.

The emotional rewards of generosity are immense. The happiness of seeing someone's face light up upon receiving a gift, the satisfaction of knowing you've made a difference, and the deeper connections formed through acts of giving all contribute to a sense of fulfillment. Whether choosing the perfect gift, donating to a worthy cause, spending time with someone or sharing your skills, the joy you experience is a reminder of the power of giving.

Though often fleeting, these moments leave lasting impressions on both the giver and the receiver, enriching lives in ways that words can scarcely capture.

4.5 LETTERS FROM THE HEART

There's a certain magic in the act of writing a letter. The way the ink flows onto paper captures thoughts and feelings that can be read and treasured over and over again. Imagine a love letter written during a long-distance relationship. Each word is chosen with care, and each line is a testament to the longing and affection that distance cannot diminish. "My dearest," it might begin, "though miles separate us, my heart is always with you."

Upon opening the letter, the recipient feels the writer's presence as if they are right there. The emotional impact of such heartfelt words is profound, providing comfort and connection in the absence of physical closeness.

Though often brief, a thank-you note can express deep appreciation in a way that spoken words sometimes cannot. Consider the joy of receiving a handwritten note after a kind gesture. It might say, "Your generosity touched my heart in ways I cannot express. Thank you for being so wonderful." The simple act of putting pen to paper to convey gratitude creates a lasting impression, making the recipient feel valued and appreciated. These letters become keepsakes, tangible reminders of the kindness and connection shared between people.

The tradition of letter writing has played a crucial role in various contexts throughout history. Soldiers exchanging letters with their families during times of war is a poignant example. These letters were lifelines, providing solace and hope amidst the chaos of conflict. A soldier might write, "I miss you all terribly, but your letters give me the strength to carry on." The family, in turn, would eagerly await each letter, finding comfort in the familiar handwriting and the news from their loved one.

Letters of apology also hold significant power, mending broken relationships and offering a path to reconciliation. A heartfelt apology letter might read, "I am deeply sorry for my actions. Please forgive me and allow us to heal and move forward together." Such letters can bridge gaps, fostering understanding and forgiveness.

Receiving and keeping letters brings immense joy. I recall my grandmother's box of love letters from her late husband. Each letter, carefully preserved, told the story of their courtship and marriage. Similarly, a collection of birthday cards kept over the years serves as a chronicle of relationships and milestones. Each card, with its personal message, is a snapshot of a moment in time, preserving the emotions and connections of that day.

Writing letters can also lead to personal growth and deeper connections. Some people write letters to themselves as a form of reflection. It's a kind of journaling. These letters, often written at significant moments, provide a way to process thoughts and emotions. A letter to oneself might begin, "Dear me, today I faced a challenge, but I learned so much about my strength and resilience." This practice can enhance self-awareness and provide a record of personal growth.

Friends who maintain a lifelong bond through regular correspondence find that letter writing strengthens their relationship. Each letter is a continuation of their ongoing conversation, a thread that weaves their lives together despite physical distance.

The power of written words to express love and gratitude is undeniable. Whether through a love letter, a thank-you note, or a letter of apology, the act of writing and receiving letters creates lasting emotional connections. In various contexts, the tradition of letter writing has bridged distances and mended relationships.

Writing letters fosters personal growth and strengthens connections, making it a practice that enriches both the writer and the recipient.

5

SIMPLE PLEASURES

When I was younger, I often visited my parents on weekends. Each morning, I woke to the comforting aroma of freshly brewed coffee wafting through the house. My parents had a ritual that was as predictable as the sunrise. They would sit at the kitchen table, sipping their coffee while reading the morning newspaper. This simple routine set the tone for the day, offering a moment of peace and reflection before the world outside demanded their attention.

5.1 MORNING COFFEE RITUALS

Morning coffee is more than just a beverage; it's a cherished ritual that provides comfort and a routine. As you pour that first cup, the steam rises, carrying with it the rich, inviting scent of freshly brewed coffee. The kitchen fills with this comforting aroma, creating a warm and welcoming atmosphere. Sitting down with a cup of coffee, you can take a moment to pause and reflect, savoring the quiet start to your day. It's a time for gathering your thoughts, planning the day, or simply enjoying a few minutes of solitude.

For many, the ritual includes reading the morning newspaper. There's something incredibly satisfying about the rustle of the pages as you turn them, sipping your coffee in between articles. The news might bring you updates from around the world, but reading it in the comfort of your home, with a steaming cup of coffee in hand, makes the experience uniquely personal and grounding. This routine becomes a cherished part of the morning, a small but significant way to connect with the world while enjoying the simple pleasure of your favorite brew.

Coffee also has a remarkable way of bringing people together. Meeting a friend at a local café for a cup is a time-honored tradition. These gatherings are more than just an opportunity to enjoy a delicious drink; they are moments of connection and conversation. Whether you're catching up on each other's lives, sharing stories, or simply enjoying quiet companionship, the act of sharing coffee creates a bond. The café setting, with its hum of activity and the comforting aroma of coffee, provides the perfect backdrop for these meaningful interactions.

For couples, morning coffee can be a special time to connect before the day begins. Sitting together, enjoying the warmth of your coffee, you can share quiet conversations and savor the peaceful moments before the hustle and bustle take over. These simple, shared experiences strengthen your connection, reminding you of the love and companionship you share. The routine of making and enjoying coffee together becomes a small but significant part of your relationship, a comforting ritual that brings you closer.

The sensory experiences associated with coffee add to its allure. The first sip of hot coffee brings a warmth that spreads through your body, waking you up and lifting your spirits. The rich and complex taste dances on your palate, offering pure enjoyment. The sound of the coffee maker percolating in the background adds to the ambiance, a familiar and comforting noise that signals the start of a new day. These sensory elements combine to create a soothing and refreshing experience, making morning coffee a beloved ritual for many.

Everyone has their unique way of enjoying coffee, adding personal touches that make it their own. Some prefer their coffee black, savoring the pure, unadulterated flavor. Others might add a splash of cream and a spoonful of sugar, creating a creamy, sweet concoction. The choices are endless, from flavored syrups to frothy milk, each variation reflecting individual preferences and tastes. Brewing methods also vary, with some favoring a traditional drip coffee maker, while others might opt for a French press or a pour-over technique. Each method brings out different nuances in the coffee, offering a new experience with every cup.

Finding a favorite blend from a local roastery can elevate the experience for those who cherish their coffee. Supporting local businesses ensures a fresh, high-quality product and adds a sense of community to your coffee ritual. Knowing that your coffee was roasted just a few miles away by people who share your passion for a good cup of joe adds a layer of satisfaction that goes beyond the beverage itself. It's a reminder of the simple pleasures of supporting and connecting with your local community.

Reflection Section: Your Morning Coffee Ritual

Take a moment to reflect on your own morning coffee ritual. That is, of course, if you drink coffee at all; not all of us do.

What makes it unique for you? Do you have a favorite blend or a special way of preparing your coffee? How does this simple pleasure set the tone for your day?

5.2 PORCH SWING CONVERSATIONS

There's something uniquely comforting about sitting on a porch swing, its gentle creak as it moves back and forth, creating a soothing rhythm. Imagine a quiet evening, the air cool and crisp, as you settle into the swing with a blanket draped over your lap. The view before you is a blooming garden, vibrant with colors and fragrant with the scent of flowers. Perhaps it's a quiet street where the occasional passerby waves hello, adding to the sense of community. This simple pleasure, the act of swinging slowly, invites a sense of tranquility and peace that's hard to find elsewhere.

Porch swings have a way of fostering meaningful conversations. Grandparents often find this spot perfect for sharing tales of their youth with grandchildren. They recount stories of simpler times, of adventures and lessons learned, their voices filled with nostalgia and wisdom. These tales, passed down through generations, create a bond between young and old, connecting them through shared history. Neighbors, too, find the porch swing an ideal place to catch up on community happenings and reminisce. Conversations flow easily, and the relaxed atmosphere encourages open and heartfelt exchanges. Memories are shared, and new ones are made, all while gently swaying back and forth.

The sensory experiences of a porch swing add to its charm. The feel of a cool evening breeze on your face is refreshing, a gentle reminder of nature's ever-present touch. Birds chirping and leaves rustling nearby create a natural symphony, a backdrop of calming, familiar sounds. With its slight movement, the swing mimics the comforting sensation of being rocked, evoking feelings of safety and relaxation. These sensory elements combine to make sitting on a porch swing a multi-faceted experience, engaging your senses in a way that soothes the mind and body.

People find various ways to enjoy their time on a porch swing, each adding their unique touch to this simple pleasure. Some might bring out a favorite book, losing themselves in the pages while gently swaying. The swing becomes a cozy reading nook, where stories come to life against the backdrop of a blooming garden or a quiet street. Others might sip on a glass of lemonade, the cool, tangy drink refreshing on a warm summer day. The swing provides the perfect setting for such simple delights, making each moment feel special and cherished.

For some, the porch swing is a place for quiet reflection. Sitting there, watching the world go by, offers a chance to pause and think. It's a time to process the day's events, plan for the future, or simply enjoy the present moment. The gentle motion of the swing, combined with the peaceful surroundings, creates an ideal environment for introspection and mindfulness. It's a space where worries can be set aside, if only for a while, and where clarity and calm can be found.

In other instances, the porch swing becomes a gathering spot for family and friends. On weekends, it might be the centerpiece of a lively gathering, with people taking turns to sit and chat. Laughter fills the air as stories are shared, creating a sense of togetherness and joy. It becomes a symbol of hospitality and warmth, inviting everyone to come together and enjoy the simple pleasure of each other's company.

So, if you are in the luxurious position of owning a porch swing, make sure you enjoy the beautiful moments it can create!

5.3 BAKING CHRISTMAS COOKIES

Every December, the anticipation of our annual cookie-baking tradition fills the air with excitement and warmth. The kitchen becomes a bustling hub of activity, each corner of the room alive with the festive spirit. The aroma of freshly baked cookies wafts through the house, mingling with the scent of pine from the Christmas tree. Christmas music plays softly in the background, setting the perfect mood for the occasion.

Family members gather around the kitchen island, ready to participate in the baking process. The counters are lined with bowls of colorful sprinkles, tubes of icing, and cookie cutters in every imaginable festive shape. It's a scene that feels like pure holiday magic.

The process begins with rolling out the dough, a task that always brings a sense of nostalgia. The kids love pressing the cookie cutters into the dough, their faces lighting up with each perfectly shaped star, tree, or gingerbread man.

Once the cookies are cut, they go into the oven, filling the kitchen with a mouthwatering aroma that makes waiting almost unbearable.

The real fun, however, starts when the cookies come out and it's time to decorate. Everyone gathers around the table, each person with their own batch of cookies to adorn. Tubes of colorful icing are passed around, and bowls of sprinkles are shared. Laughter fills the room as we create unique designs, each cookie a small work of art. The younger ones, their fingers sticky with icing, delight in the freedom to be creative.

Specific memories and traditions make this activity even more special, like a grandson making his own batch of cookies for the first time. His eyes sparkled with pride as he carefully placed each cookie on the baking sheet. That day, he learned how to bake and the joy of creating something with his hands.

Another cherished memory is the special recipe for gingerbread cookies that has been passed down through generations. My grandmother taught it to my mother, who taught it to us, and now we share it with children and grandchildren. The smell of those gingerbread cookies baking in the oven instantly transports me back to my own childhood, filled with the warmth and love of family.

Giving homemade cookies as gifts has become a beloved tradition in its own right. Every year, we package up boxes of cookies to give to neighbors and friends. The act of giving, of sharing something we made with our own hands, adds a layer of meaning to the holiday season. It's a simple gesture, but it brings so much joy to both the giver and the receiver. I recall the delight on our neighbor's face when we handed her a box of freshly baked cookies, each one carefully decorated and packed with love. These moments of giving and sharing strengthen our sense of community and remind us of the true spirit of the holidays.

The lasting impact of this tradition goes beyond the cookies themselves. They become a symbol of family unity and love, a tangible representation of the time and effort we put into creating something together. Each year, as the holiday season approaches, there is a sense of anticipation and excitement for the cookie-baking day. It's a cherished part of our holiday celebrations, a tradition that brings us together and fills our home with warmth and joy. The activity has become a cornerstone of our family traditions, one that we look forward to every year.

As the years go by, this tradition is passed down to future generations. The younger ones, who once watched and helped, grew up to take on more significant roles in the baking process. They learn the recipes, the techniques, and the joy of creating something with love. The tradition evolves and adapts, but the core values of family, love, and togetherness remain unchanged.

5.4 THE CHARM OF OLD MOVIES

There's a special kind of joy in finding an old favorite film on TV. The excitement builds as you recognize the familiar opening credits, a gateway to a nostalgic journey. You rush to the kitchen to prepare a bowl of popcorn, the kernels popping rhythmically in the microwave. The scent of buttery popcorn fills the room, adding to the anticipation. You settle into your favorite chair, remote in hand, ready to be transported back in time. The ritual of making popcorn and finding a cozy spot creates a sense of comfort and familiarity, setting the stage for a delightful experience.

Old movies have a unique ability to connect us to past eras and evoke fond memories. Watching these films brings back the excitement of seeing them for the first time in a theater. You recall the thrill of the big screen, the buzz of the audience, and the magic of the movie unfolding before your eyes. The fashion and cultural references of the time period add another layer of nostalgia. The elegant dresses, tailored suits, and classic cars transport you to a bygone era, reminding you of a different time in your life. Each scene becomes a portal to cherished memories, bringing the past to life in vivid detail.

The sensory experiences of watching an old movie are part of what makes it so enjoyable. The black-and-white visuals have a timeless quality, and their simplicity adds to the charm. The vintage film scores, with their sweeping melodies and dramatic crescendos, create an emotional backdrop that enhances the storytelling. There's something nostalgic about the sound of a film projector whirring or the clicks of a VHS tape being inserted into the player. These familiar sounds and sights evoke a sense of comfort and warmth, making the experience of watching an old movie feel like revisiting an old friend.

People enjoy old movies in various settings and company types, each adding a unique flavor to the experience. A classic film night with family can be a wonderful way to bond and share memories. Everyone gathers in the living room, the lights dim, and the movie starts playing. Laughter and gasps fill the room as you watch together, creating a shared experience that brings you closer. On a rainy day, a solo movie marathon is the perfect way to spend a cozy afternoon. You curl up on the couch with a blanket and a cup of tea and lose yourself in a series of beloved classics. The rain tapping against the window adds to the ambiance, making the experience even more special.

The charm of old movies lies in their ability to transport us to another time and place while evoking powerful emotions and memories. Each viewing is a chance to relive the magic of the past and reconnect with the stories and characters that have touched our hearts. Whether watched alone or with loved ones, old movies offer a comforting escape, a reminder of the simple pleasures that bring joy to our lives.

As we reflect on the simple pleasures that enrich our days, it's clear that these moments of comfort and connection play a vital role in our well-being. From morning coffee rituals to porch swing conversations and the joy of baking Christmas cookies, each activity offers a unique way to connect with ourselves and others.

In the next chapter, we will explore the importance of community and friendship, delving into the stories and experiences that highlight the power of human connection. From local diner gatherings to the impact of volunteering together, we'll uncover the ways in which our relationships shape and enrich our lives.

TELL OTHERS ABOUT IT BY LEAVING A REVIEW!

Have you enjoyed reading this book so far?

If so, the best you can do is tell others about it by leaving a review!

Your opinion matters...

Your help is essential so others find this book and benefit from it, too.

As a self-published author, your feedback is my lifeline and essential for reaching more people who are looking for books they enjoy.

Please take a moment to leave a review on Amazon.

It's quick and easy:

1. Find the book on Amazon, or even faster click your 'Returns & Orders' button
2. Scroll down and click on "Write a product review."
3. Share your thoughts and click "Submit."

Or, simply scan the QR code below to go straight to the review page.

Thank you for your support and for helping others discover this book!

Now, let's continue to the next chapter.

6

COMMUNITY AND FRIENDSHIP

The local diner has always held a special charm for me. It's a place where time seems to slow down, and the hustle and bustle of the outside world fades away. Walking through the door, you're greeted by the familiar clink of coffee cups and the warm aroma of freshly brewed coffee. The diner is more than just a place to grab a meal; it's a community hub where friendships are forged, news is shared, and life's milestones are celebrated.

6.1 THE LOCAL DINER GATHERING

The morning rush at the diner is a sight to behold. Regulars take their usual seats, greeting each other with nods and smiles. There's a comforting predictability to it, a sense of belonging that's hard to find elsewhere. The staff, familiar with each customer's preferences, engage in friendly banter, asking about grandchildren or recent vacations. The diner is alive with conversations, each table a little world of its own.

You can hear the sizzle of bacon on the griddle, which promises a hearty breakfast. The clinking of coffee cups and silverware creates a soothing rhythm, a backdrop to the diverse conversations that fill the room. At one table, a group of friends might be sharing the latest news about their families, while at another, a heated debate about local politics or the performance of the town's sports team ensues. The diner is a melting pot of topics, where everyone's voice is heard, and every story is valued.

The diner's sensory experiences are what make it so memorable. The smell of fresh pancakes mingles with the scent of brewing coffee, creating an inviting atmosphere. Seeing a waitress expertly balancing plates as she weaves through the tables is a familiar and comforting scene. The sounds of laughter, conversation, and the occasional clatter of dishes blend together, creating a symphony of community life.

The diner is also a place of support and celebration. Birthdays are often marked with a special breakfast, complete with candles stuck into a stack of pancakes. Friends gather around, singing and clapping, making the celebrant feel cherished and loved. In times of difficulty, the diner becomes a sanctuary. I recall a time when a regular was going through a tough period. The staff and patrons rallied around, offering words of comfort, a listening ear, and sometimes even a hug. It was a beautiful reminder of the power of community and the strength found in shared bonds.

Imagine a morning when you find yourself at your favorite booth, the one by the window with the perfect view of the bustling street outside. Your closest friends join you, each bringing their unique humor and wisdom. The conversation flows easily, moving from light-hearted banter to deeper discussions about life. The waitress, who knows you all by name, brings over your usual orders without needing to ask. In these moments, you realize the diner is more than just a place to eat; it's a cornerstone of your social life, a place where you feel seen and understood.

Every diner has its regulars, those familiar faces that become like family. There's Joe, who always has a story to tell, and Mary, whose laugh is infectious. Over time, you get to know their quirks, habits, and likes and dislikes. These friendships, formed over countless cups of coffee and shared meals, become an integral part of your life. The diner is a place where you can be yourself, where your presence is valued, and where you are part of a larger community.

The local diner is a microcosm of community life, a place where bonds are formed and connections are deepened. It's a setting filled with sensory delights, from the smells and sounds to the sights and tastes. It's a place of support and celebration, where milestones are marked, and challenges are faced together. The diner is a testament to the power of community, where you can find comfort, joy, and a sense of belonging.

6.2 THE BOOK CLUB THAT SAVED A LIFE

When Jane moved to a new retirement community, she felt a profound sense of isolation. Gone were the familiar faces and daily routines that had comforted her for years. One afternoon, while exploring her new surroundings, she noticed a colorful flyer pinned to the community bulletin board. It advertised a local book club, inviting residents to join for a discussion of that month's selection. Jane hesitated but then thought, "Why not?" She had always loved reading, and perhaps this could be a way to meet new people.

Jane attended her first meeting with a mix of excitement and nervousness. She was greeted with warm smiles and welcoming words as she walked into the cozy living room where the group gathered. The book club members, a diverse group of seniors, immediately made her feel at home. They introduced themselves, shared a bit about their favorite books, and asked Jane about her reading preferences. The atmosphere was inviting, and Jane quickly realized she had found something special.

The discussions were lively and engaging, covering a wide range of topics, from the book's themes to personal anecdotes. Jane found herself looking forward to these meetings, where she enjoyed stimulating conversations and began forming meaningful connections with her fellow members. They discussed everything from classic literature to contemporary bestsellers, each member bringing their unique perspective to the table. Jane felt a renewed sense of purpose and joy, knowing she had found a place where she belonged.

One evening, after a particularly engaging discussion about "The Nightingale" by Kristin Hannah, Jane felt an unexpected tightness in her chest. She brushed it off, thinking it was just the excitement of the evening. But the discomfort persisted, and by morning, it had worsened. Jane confided in her new friends at the book club; their response was immediate and heartfelt. Two members insisted on accompanying her to the doctor, while others offered to bring meals and check in on her regularly.

The diagnosis was a minor heart issue, but the support from her book club friends was anything but minor. They rallied around her, providing emotional and practical assistance that made all the difference. One member, a retired nurse, explained the medical jargon and helped Jane understand her treatment plan. Another member, who lived nearby, took her to follow-up appointments, ensuring she never felt alone. Their kindness and support turned a frightening experience into a manageable one, deeply touching Jane's heart.

As Jane recovered, she reflected on how much the book club had come to mean to her. It was more than just a group of people who shared a love for reading; it had become a lifeline, a source of deep friendships and unwavering support. The book club meetings continued, and Jane felt a growing sense of community and belonging. Each discussion, each shared laugh, and each act of kindness strengthened the bonds between the members, creating a tight-knit, supportive community.

The book club's impact extended beyond Jane's personal experience. The members celebrated each other's milestones, from birthdays to anniversaries, and supported one another through life's challenges. They organized outings to local literary events, further enriching their shared love for books. For Jane, the book club transformed her retirement experience, providing her a new sense of purpose, joy, and connection.

Through the simple act of reading and discussing books, Jane found herself surrounded by friends who cared deeply for her well-being. The book club saved her life, offering companionship and a profound sense of community and belonging. The friendships formed within the club were genuine and lasting, proving that even in new and unfamiliar surroundings, it is possible to find a place where you truly belong.

6.3 NEIGHBORS HELPING NEIGHBORS

Living in a close-knit neighborhood can be a truly wonderful experience. Knowing your neighbors well brings a unique sense of community and mutual support. Picture this: the sound of a lawnmower humming next door as a neighbor helps with yard work, the smell of freshly cut grass filling the air. It's not uncommon to see folks lending a hand with home repairs, whether it's fixing a leaky faucet or painting a fence. These acts of kindness and cooperation create a tapestry of goodwill, making everyone feel more connected and supported.

Sharing the surplus from garden harvests is another delightful tradition in many neighborhoods. Imagine receiving a basket of ripe tomatoes or freshly picked herbs from the neighbor down the street. These small gestures foster a spirit of generosity and camaraderie. It's the kind of place where you might find a jar of homemade jam left on your doorstep, a simple yet heartwarming reminder that you're part of a community that cares.

Looking out for each other is a cornerstone of a supportive neighborhood. A profound peace of mind comes from knowing your neighbors are there for you. Checking in on elderly or ill neighbors becomes second nature, ensuring they have everything they need and aren't feeling isolated. Organizing neighborhood watch programs adds an extra layer of security, with everyone keeping an eye out for each other. This sense of vigilance and care creates an environment where residents feel safe and valued.

Informal gatherings and spontaneous interactions are the lifeblood of a vibrant community. Picture impromptu barbecues where everyone brings a dish to share, the aroma of grilled burgers and hot dogs mingling with the laughter of friends and neighbors. Kids play together, their joyful shouts echoing as they chase each other around the yard, while parents chat and catch up on each other's lives. These casual, everyday moments strengthen bonds and build lasting friendships.

The emotional impact of living in a close-knit community is profound. A deep sense of belonging and security comes from knowing you're part of something bigger than yourself. Neighbors rally together during a crisis, offering support and comfort when needed. Whether it's a family facing a medical emergency or someone dealing with a personal loss, the community steps in, providing meals, running errands, or simply being there to listen. These acts of solidarity create a safety net that makes life's challenges more bearable.

Shared celebrations and achievements bring immense joy to the community. Think about the excitement of a block party where everyone gathers to celebrate a holiday or a special occasion. There's music, dancing, and the delicious smell of homemade dishes. People share stories, laugh, and create new memories together. These celebrations are more than just social events; they're a testament to the community's bonds. They provide opportunities to acknowledge and celebrate each other's successes, reinforcing the sense of unity and shared purpose.

A long time ago, one memorable occasion was when our neighborhood came together to help a family rebuild after a house fire. The outpouring of support was overwhelming. Neighbors donated clothes, furniture, and money, while others offered their time and skills to help with the rebuilding process. It was a powerful reminder of the strength and resilience of our community. The family, though deeply affected by the loss, found comfort in the collective support and love of their neighbors. It was a testament to the power of community and the difference that collective efforts can make.

Living in a neighborhood where people genuinely care for one another is a gift. The acts of kindness and cooperation, the peace of mind that comes from looking out for each other, the informal gatherings, and the emotional impact of a close-knit community all contribute to a rich and fulfilling life. These experiences remind us that we are not alone and are part of a network of support and friendship that enhances our lives in immeasurable ways.

6.4 THE REUNION OF OLD FRIENDS

Tom and Robert were inseparable during their childhood. Growing up in the same neighborhood, they spent countless hours riding their bikes, playing baseball, and dreaming about the future. Life, however, had other plans. As they grew older, circumstances pulled them in different directions. Tom moved across the country for college, and Robert joined the military. Over the years, they lost touch, each consumed by their own lives and responsibilities. Decades passed, and the memories of those carefree days faded into the background, replaced by the demands of adulthood. Yet, the bond they shared in their youth remained a cherished part of their past.

One day, while sorting through an old box of photos, Tom stumbled upon a picture of him and Robert from their high school graduation. The nostalgia hit him hard, and he couldn't help but wonder what had become of his old friend. Determined to reconnect, he decided to organize a reunion. He reached out to mutual acquaintances and scoured social media, hoping to find a way to get in touch with Robert. After weeks of searching, he found Robert's contact information through a mutual friend. With excitement and a hint of nervousness, Tom sent Robert a message, proposing a reunion.

The weeks leading up to the reunion were filled with anticipation. Tom and Robert exchanged messages, reminiscing about the good old days and catching up on the years they had missed. They coordinated travel plans, deciding on a weekend when both could take a break from their busy lives. As the date approached, Tom found himself thinking more and more about their childhood adventures, the shared laughter, and the dreams they once had. The anticipation built up, and he couldn't wait to see his old friend again.

When the day of the reunion finally arrived, emotions ran high. As Tom waited at the agreed meeting spot—a quaint café in their old neighborhood—his mind raced with memories. The moment Robert walked through the door, both men were overcome with emotion. They embraced, tears of joy streaming down their faces as if no time had passed at all. The café, filled with the hum of conversations and the clinking of coffee cups, became a backdrop to their heartfelt reunion. They spent hours sharing memories, laughing at old jokes, and catching up on each other's lives. Tom had brought along old photographs, and they pored over them, each picture sparking a flood of memories. They revisited their old haunts, the baseball field where they had spent countless summer afternoons, and the treehouse they had built with their own hands. Every place held a story, a piece of their shared history that they joyfully relived.

The reunion had a profound impact on both men. They realized how much they had missed each other and vowed not to let so much time pass again. They decided to stay in regular contact, planning future get-togethers and even family vacations. The sense of fulfillment and joy from rekindling their friendship was palpable.

It wasn't just about reliving the past, creating new memories, and strengthening their bond. The reunion also served as an inspiration to others in their community. Hearing about Tom and Robert's story, many people began reaching out to old friends, organizing their own reunions, and reconnecting with those they had lost touch with over the years. The ripple effect of their reunion brought a renewed sense of community and belonging to their neighborhood.

Tom and Robert's reunion is a testament to the enduring power of friendship. Despite the years and the distance, the bond they shared in their youth was still strong. The joy and fulfillment they found in reconnecting reminded them—and everyone around them—that true friendships can withstand the test of time. Their story is a beautiful reminder of the importance of cherishing our relationships and making an effort to reconnect with those who have touched our lives in meaningful ways.

6.5 VOLUNTEERING TOGETHER

Volunteering brings a profound sense of purpose and fulfillment. Imagine organizing a food drive with your community. You gather donations, sort through canned goods, and prepare packages for families in need. The collective effort transforms a simple act into a powerful force for good. Each box you pack represents a meal for someone who might otherwise go hungry. Distributing these donations, you see the gratitude in recipients' eyes, and it warms your heart. Participating in community clean-up events offers a different kind of satisfaction. Armed with gloves and trash bags, you and your neighbors work side by side, beautifying parks and public spaces. The physical labor, though tiring, leaves you with a sense of accomplishment as you see the immediate impact of your efforts. These collective actions improve your surroundings and foster a deeper connection to your community.

The social connections formed through volunteering are invaluable. A unique camaraderie develops when you work together towards a common goal. As you bond over shared experiences, you celebrate each milestone and achievement as a team. Whether it's reaching a fundraising target or completing a challenging project, these shared successes create lasting memories. You find yourself forming friendships with people you might never have met otherwise. The teamwork involved in volunteering fosters a sense of unity and belonging. You start to look forward to these events, not just for the cause but for the joy of working alongside friends who share your passion for making a difference.

Volunteering offers a diverse range of opportunities to give back. Mentoring youth or tutoring students provides a chance to share your knowledge and experience. Guiding young people through their academic journey or helping them discover their potential is incredibly rewarding. Supporting local shelters and food banks is another way to make a meaningful impact. Whether you're serving meals, organizing donations, or simply offering a listening ear, your efforts provide much-needed support to those facing difficult times. Each volunteer role has unique challenges and rewards, allowing you to find a cause that resonates with your values and interests.

The long-term impact of volunteering extends beyond immediate benefits. Community facilities and resources often see significant improvements thanks to dedicated volunteers. Your efforts might help renovate a community center, build a playground, or create a community garden. These enhancements enrich the lives of everyone in the neighborhood, providing spaces for relaxation, recreation, and socialization. Volunteering also offers personal growth and the development of new skills. Depending on the tasks at hand, you can learn project management, public speaking, or carpentry. These skills enhance your volunteer work and enrich your personal and professional life.

One memorable experience I had was volunteering at a local shelter. Initially, I felt apprehensive, unsure of what to expect. But as I served meals and listened to the stories of those I met, I realized the profound impact of simply being present. The gratitude and resilience of the people I encountered left a lasting impression. It was a humbling experience that reminded me of the importance of compassion and empathy.

Another time, I participated in a mentoring program for high school students. Seeing my mentee graduate and pursue higher education was one of the proudest moments of my life. It reinforced my belief in the power of guidance and support in shaping young lives.

As we reflect on the power of community and friendship, let's turn our focus to the next chapter, where we explore the rich tapestry of cultural traditions that add depth and meaning to our lives.

7

CULTURAL TRADITIONS

One year, my family and I decided to spend Christmas in Germany. We wanted to experience the holiday season in a different culture, and Germany, with its long-standing traditions and festive spirit, seemed like the perfect destination. The moment we arrived, we were engulfed by the magic of the season. Twinkling lights adorned every corner, and the aroma of freshly baked gingerbread filled the air.

7.1 CHRISTMAS AROUND THE WORLD

Christmas is celebrated in countless ways around the globe, each country adding its unique touch to the holiday. One of Italy's most cherished traditions is the Feast of the Seven Fishes, or "La Vigilia." On Christmas Eve, Italian families gather to share a meal with seven different seafood dishes, a practice rooted in the Roman Catholic tradition of abstaining from meat the night before Christmas. The table is laden with delicacies like baccalà (salted cod), calamari, and clams, each dish prepared with love and passed down through generations. The meal celebrates family and faith, bringing everyone together in a spirit of generosity and togetherness.

Meanwhile, on the other side of the world, Australians celebrate Christmas with a distinctly summery twist. Instead of the cold, snowy landscapes many associate with the holiday, Australians enjoy warm weather and sunshine in the midst of summer. Christmas Day often involves beach barbecues, where families and friends gather to grill fresh seafood and meats. Picture the scene: people in swimsuits and Santa hats, the scent of sizzling prawns and sausages in the air, and the sound of waves crashing nearby. It's a vibrant and relaxed celebration, reflecting the laid-back Australian lifestyle. The beach becomes a festive gathering place where laughter and joy are shared as freely as the sunshine.

In Puerto Rico, the holiday season is marked by the lively tradition of parranda. These are musical processions, similar to caroling, where groups of friends and family move from house to house, playing instruments and singing traditional Christmas songs. The music is infectious, with rhythms that make you want to dance and sing along. The festivities often start late at night and continue into the early morning hours. Hosts welcome the parranderos with food and drinks, creating a warm and festive atmosphere. The celebration is a testament to the Puerto Rican spirit of community and joy, where everyone is invited to join in the fun.

The sensory experiences of Christmas celebrations are universal, yet each culture adds unique flavors and sounds. In Germany, the aroma of freshly baked gingerbread, or Lebkuchen, fills the air. These spicy-sweet cookies are a holiday staple, often decorated with intricate designs and enjoyed with a hot cup of Glühwein, a mulled wine that warms you from the inside out. The colorful Christmas markets, or Weihnachtsmärkte, are a feast for the eyes. Stalls brimming with handmade crafts, twinkling lights, and festive decorations create a magical atmosphere. The carolers singing in the town square add to the enchantment, making it feel like you've entered a Christmas fairy tale.

Despite the differences in customs and traditions, certain themes unite Christmas celebrations around the world. The act of gift-giving is a universal expression of love and generosity. In many cultures, presents are exchanged on Christmas Eve or Christmas morning, each carefully chosen gift a token of affection and thoughtfulness. Family gatherings are another common thread. Whether it's an Italian family sharing the Feast of the Seven Fishes, Australians enjoying a beach barbecue, or Puerto Ricans hosting a parranda, the holiday season is a time to come together, share meals, and create lasting memories.

Learning new traditions and incorporating them into our own celebrations has become a cherished part of our Christmas experience. Each year, we try to introduce something new, inspired by the customs we've encountered on our travels. One year, we adopted the German tradition of hiding a pickle ornament in the Christmas tree. The finder receives an extra gift, adding an element of fun and surprise to the holiday. Another year, we made it a point to include some traditional Puerto Rican music in our celebrations, bringing a bit of the parranda spirit to our family gathering. These additions keep our celebrations fresh and exciting while also honoring the diverse ways people around the world celebrate this special time of year.

7.2 HARVEST FESTIVALS

Harvest festivals are special in many cultures, symbolizing gratitude and community. These celebrations mark the end of the growing season when the hard work of planting and tending crops pays off with bountiful harvests. In the United States, Thanksgiving is the most well-known harvest festival. Celebrated on the fourth Thursday of November, it brings families together to share a feast. The origins of Thanksgiving date back to 1621, when Pilgrims and Native Americans gathered for a meal to give thanks for the harvest. Today, the holiday continues to embody gratitude, with tables laden with turkey, stuffing, and pumpkin pie.

In China and a number of surrounding countries, the Mid-Autumn Festival is a major harvest celebration. It is held on the 15th day of the eighth lunar month. The festival is a time for families to gather and enjoy mooncakes, a sweet pastry filled with lotus seed paste or red bean paste. Lantern parades are also a highlight, with children and adults carrying colorful lanterns in various shapes and sizes. Seeing these glowing lanterns lighting up the night sky is truly magical, creating a sense of unity and joy. The festival is steeped in legend, with stories of the moon goddess Chang'e adding a layer of mystique to the celebrations.

In India, Pongal is a multi-day harvest festival celebrated mainly in the southern state of Tamil Nadu. It usually takes place in mid-January and is dedicated to the sun god, Surya. The festival includes traditional dances, elaborate feasts, and the preparation of a special dish called Pongal, made from freshly harvested rice, milk, and jaggery. Homes are decorated with colorful kolam designs, intricate patterns made from rice flour. The air is filled with the sounds of folk music and the aroma of delicious food, creating an atmosphere of festivity and gratitude. It's a time for giving thanks for the harvest and seeking blessings for future prosperity.

The sensory experiences of harvest festivals are unforgettable. Picture a cool autumn evening with a bonfire crackling in the center of a community gathering. The smell of burning wood mingles with the scents of various harvest dishes. In the United States, the aroma of pumpkin pie baking in the oven, spiced with cinnamon and nutmeg, fills homes with a warm and inviting scent. The sweet smell of Pongal cooking in clay pots over open fires in India adds to the festive atmosphere. Folk music and laughter echo through the air, creating a symphony of joy and celebration.

Many American families take an annual trip to a local pumpkin patch and corn maze. They spend the day picking pumpkins, navigating the maze, and enjoying hayrides. The crisp autumn air and the vibrant colors of the changing leaves make it a perfect day out. Then, they return home with the pumpkins, ready to carve them into jack-o'-lanterns for Halloween.

Participating in a community harvest feast is another cherished memory for many. The neighborhood comes together for a potluck dinner, with everyone bringing a dish made from seasonal produce. The sense of community and shared gratitude make these events truly special.

In these ways, harvest festivals worldwide highlight the importance of gratitude and community spirit. They bring people together to celebrate the fruits of their labor, share meals, and create memories.

7.3 TRADITIONAL CRAFTING

Traditional crafts hold a special place in our hearts and cultures. They are more than just art forms; they are a living testament to the skills and artistry passed down through generations. Take, for instance, the weaving of baskets in Native American cultures. Each basket is a masterpiece, intricately designed with patterns that tell stories and hold significant meanings. The knowledge of basket weaving is often passed from elders to the younger generation, ensuring that these traditions endure. The process is meticulous, requiring patience and precision. Each strand of material is carefully chosen and woven, creating a functional yet beautiful piece of art that reflects the heritage and identity of the community.

In Indonesia, the art of creating batik designs is both a cultural and artistic treasure. Batik involves a wax-resist dyeing technique, where intricate patterns are drawn with hot wax on fabric before dyeing it. The areas covered in wax resist the dye, resulting in stunning, multicolored designs once the wax is removed. This craft requires a keen eye for detail and a steady hand. The artisans who practice batik often start learning as children, perfecting their skills over years of practice. The vibrant patterns and colors of batik fabrics are a visual feast, each piece telling a story of tradition, creativity, and cultural pride.

The process and techniques involved in traditional crafts are as fascinating as the final products themselves. Hand-weaving textiles, for example, is a labor-intensive process that demands skill and creativity. The weaver carefully selects threads, often dyed with natural pigments, and meticulously interlaces them on a loom. Each movement of the shuttle and each tightening of the threads contribute to the creation of a unique and intricate pattern. The rhythm of the weaving process is almost meditative, a dance of hands and threads that results in a beautiful fabric ingrained with cultural significance.

Traditional pottery making is another craft that showcases incredible precision and artistry. The potter's wheel spins as the artisan shapes a lump of clay into a vessel. The feel of the clay as it responds to the potter's touch is a tactile experience that connects the artist to the earth. Each piece of pottery goes through multiple stages, from shaping and refining to drying and firing. The final product is a testament to the potter's skill and patience, each piece unique in its form and decoration. The intricate designs and glazes applied to the pottery reflect cultural motifs and historical influences, making each piece a work of art.

The sensory experiences of crafting are deeply enriching. Imagine the feel of clay being shaped on a pottery wheel, its cool, smooth texture yielding to your hands. The scent of wet earth mingles with the sound of the wheel turning, creating a sensory symphony that grounds you in the moment. The vibrant colors of hand-dyed fabrics catch the eye, each hue a testament to the natural materials used in the dyeing process. The tactile sensation of weaving threads through a loom, the slight resistance as the fibers interlock, creates a physical connection to the craft. These sensory elements make traditional crafting a deeply immersive and satisfying experience.

The women in my family learned to knit from my grandmother. She had a way of making the needles dance, creating intricate patterns with ease. Sitting around her, they all fumbled with the yarn, fingers clumsy and unsure. But she was patient, guiding everyone's hands and showing them the rhythm of knitting. The process was soothing, and the repetitive motions and the soft click of the needles created a sense of calm. Each stitch was a small victory, a step toward creating something tangible and beautiful. The joy of completing a first scarf was immense, not just because of the finished product but because of the time they spent with their grandmother and the skills she passed on.

Another memorable experience was joining a community workshop to learn about traditional woodworking. The workshop was filled with the scent of fresh wood and the sound of tools in use. Under the guidance of a skilled craftsman, I learned how to carve and shape wood, transforming a simple block into a decorative piece. The process required focus and precision, but the satisfaction of seeing the final product made it all worthwhile. The camaraderie among the participants, sharing tips and encouraging each other, made the experience even more rewarding. The workshop taught me new skills and fostered a sense of community and connection.

Traditional crafts are more than just hobbies; they are a way to connect with our heritage and create something meaningful with our hands. They teach us patience, precision, and the joy of creating. Each piece we craft carries a part of us, a reflection of our efforts and creativity. Whether weaving a basket, creating a batik design, or shaping clay on a pottery wheel, traditional crafts offer a rich and fulfilling experience that connects us to our past and enriches our present. The skills and artistry involved in these crafts are a testament to the enduring power of human creativity and cultural heritage.

7.4 CELEBRATING HERITAGE

There's a special kind of joy in celebrating cultural heritage. It's a time when people come together to honor their roots, express pride in their identity, and share traditions passed down through generations.

Heritage festivals are a perfect example of this. Picture a sunny afternoon where the streets are alive with traditional music and dance sounds. Parades wind their way through neighborhoods, each float a vibrant display of national or ethnic pride. The energy is infectious, drawing everyone into the celebration. It's not just about looking back; it's about feeling connected to something bigger than yourself, a shared history that binds a community together.

During St. Patrick's Day celebrations, Irish step dancing and music take center stage. The rapid, rhythmic movements of the dancers, their feet tapping in perfect unison, create a mesmerizing spectacle. The music, often played on traditional instruments like the fiddle and tin whistle, adds a lively backdrop to the festivities. The streets are filled with people dressed in green, shamrocks pinned to their clothes, embodying the spirit of Ireland. It's a day when everyone, Irish or not, feels a sense of kinship and joy, celebrating the rich cultural heritage of the Emerald Isle.

Kwanzaa, celebrated by African American communities, is another powerful example. The rhythmic beats of African drums echo through the air, accompanied by storytelling sessions that recount the history and struggles of African ancestors. These stories are more than just tales; they are lessons in resilience, strength, and unity. The vibrant colors of Kwanzaa decorations, the red, black, and green, symbolize the blood, land, and people of Africa. The celebrations foster a sense of pride and connection, reminding participants of their cultural roots and the importance of community.

Heritage celebrations are a feast for the senses. The costumes worn during parades and dances are often elaborate and colorful, each telling a story. Imagine the swirl of a flamenco dancer's dress, the intricate embroidery on a traditional Chinese qipao, or the beadwork on a Native American regalia. These visual elements, combined with the sounds of traditional music and the scents of heritage dishes being prepared, create an immersive experience. The rich flavors of these dishes, whether it's a spicy Jamaican jerk chicken, a savory Italian pasta, or a sweet Greek baklava, add another layer of enjoyment to the festivities.

Friends of mine participated in a cultural heritage parade. They wanted to embrace their Scottish roots, donning kilts and sashes in their clan's tartan. The parade route was lined with spectators, all eager to see the various cultural displays. Bagpipes played in the background, their haunting melodies filling the air. As they marched, they felt a deep sense of pride and connection to their heritage. The day ended with a traditional Scottish feast, complete with haggis, neeps, and tatties.

Cooking traditional dishes for heritage celebrations is a cherished ritual in many families. It's a way to connect with the past and pass on cultural knowledge to the next generation. Friends of mine have a grandmother who taught them how to make pierogi, a traditional Polish dumpling. They'd spend hours in the kitchen, rolling out dough, filling it with potatoes and cheese, and then boiling and frying the dumplings to perfection. The process is as much about the stories she told—about her childhood in Poland and the dish's significance—as it was about the cooking itself. These moments created a bridge between generations, preserving the heritage by simply sharing a meal.

Heritage celebrations, with their music, dance, food, and stories, offer a rich tapestry of experiences that connect us to our roots and to each other. They remind us of our origins and values that have shaped us. As we celebrate our heritage, we honor the past while enriching our present. These traditions, whether they involve a grand parade, a family feast, or the sharing of stories, are a testament to the enduring power of cultural identity and community. They bring us together, fostering a sense of belonging and pride transcending time and place.

As we move on to the next chapter, let's carry forward the spirit of connection and community these cultural traditions inspire.

8

PERSONAL TRIUMPHS

One of my family members, in her early sixties, found herself facing a long-standing fear that had lingered since childhood: the fear of water and swimming. Watching her grandchildren splash around in the pool, the laughter echoing in the summer air, she felt a pang of regret. She wanted to join them, to share in their joy, but the water seemed like an insurmountable barrier. It was then that she made a decision that would change her life. She decided to learn to swim at the age of sixty-two. This personal triumph became an often repeated story for others who found themselves in similar life situations.

8.1 LEARNING TO SWIM AT 62

The decision to learn to swim was not made easily. It required confronting a fear that had been with her for as long as she could remember. She had always felt a sense of unease around water, a lingering fear that kept her on the shore while others enjoyed the waves. But watching her grandchildren, she realized she didn't want to miss out on these precious moments. She wanted to be a part of their world, to share in their laughter and play. Her determination to overcome this fear and join them in the pool motivated her.

Taking the first step was daunting. She enrolled in swimming lessons at the local community center, which offered a welcoming and supportive environment. And I was with her for the first lessons, for moral support. Walking into the pool area for the first time, she felt a mix of anxiety and excitement. The smell of chlorine and the sound of water splashing were both foreign and familiar. The instructor, a patient and encouraging woman named Lisa, greeted her with a warm smile. "We're going to take it one step at a time," she assured her, her calm demeanor helping to ease the nerves. She had seen others in the same situation.

The learning process was filled with challenges. The first lesson focused on getting comfortable in the water, which seemed simple but incredibly difficult for her. Learning to float was particularly challenging. The sensation of letting go and trusting the water to support her was terrifying. She struggled with the breathing techniques, often feeling panicked and out of breath. Lisa was always there, offering gentle guidance and encouragement. "You're doing great," she would say, her voice steady and reassuring. Each small victory felt monumental, like finally floating for a few seconds.

Family support played a crucial role in this journey. At a later stage, siblings, children, and grandchildren cheered her on, their enthusiasm infectious. They would come to the pool to watch her lessons, their presence providing a comforting sense of familiarity. Their cheers and claps when she managed to swim a few strokes were incredibly motivating. Her husband, too, was a pillar of support, always encouraging her to keep going, even when she felt like giving up. Their belief fueled her determination to succeed.

As the weeks went by, she began to see progress. The fear that had once seemed insurmountable started to diminish. I remember the day she successfully swam a full lap for the first time. The feeling of accomplishment was overwhelming. She emerged from the water, breathless and exhilarated, greeted by my family's cheers and the instructor's proud smile. It was a moment of triumph, a testament to the power of determination and support. The newfound confidence she gained from this achievement extended beyond the pool, influencing other areas of her life.

Joining a senior swim club was the next step in her journey. The club was a wonderful community of like-minded individuals, each with their own stories and motivations. They met regularly, not just to swim but to socialize and support each other. The camaraderie and friendships that formed there enriched her life in unexpected ways. They celebrated each other's successes, whether it was mastering a new stroke or simply showing up for practice.

Learning to swim at sixty-two was more than just acquiring a new skill. It was about overcoming a lifelong fear, finding the courage to step out of the comfort zone, and embracing new experiences. It was about the joy of joining grandchildren in the pool and sharing their laughter and play. It was about the support and encouragement from family and friends, and the sense of accomplishment and newfound confidence that came with each small victory. This journey taught us that it's never too late to learn something new, face our fears, and discover new strengths within ourselves.

8.2 THE MARATHON RUNNER

It all started with a conversation over coffee. My friend, Susan, casually mentioned her recent marathon experience, her eyes sparkling with the thrill of it. She described the rush of adrenaline, the camaraderie among runners, and the sheer sense of accomplishment as she crossed the finish line. Her story ignited something in me. I had recently entered early retirement and was looking for a new challenge, something that would push my limits and give me a sense of purpose. Running a marathon seemed like the perfect goal. It wasn't just the physical challenge; it was about proving to myself that I could do it, that age was just a number. And I had some running experience, just not running a marathon...

The decision to run a marathon was the beginning of a rigorous training regimen. I started by researching training plans, each one more daunting than the last. I settled on a schedule that balanced running with strength training and rest days. The first few weeks were the hardest. My body protested every step, muscles I didn't know I had ached, and there were days when I questioned my sanity. But with each run, I felt a little stronger, a little more capable. I adjusted my diet, focusing on foods fueling my body and aiding recovery. Long runs on weekends became a test of physical and mental endurance. There were times when fatigue set in, and I had to dig deep to keep going. But each completed run was a victory, a step closer to the goal.

The support network I built was invaluable. I joined a local running group, a diverse collection of individuals, each with their own reasons for running. We met several times a week, and our shared goal was creating a bond transcending age and background. The group provided motivation, accountability, and a sense of community. We celebrated each other's milestones and offered encouragement on tough days. My family also played a crucial role. They cheered me on during training runs and volunteered at water stations on race day, their presence a constant source of motivation.

Race day arrived with a mix of excitement and nerves. The starting line was a sea of runners, each one focused on the journey ahead. The energy was palpable, a collective anticipation that hung in the air. The first few miles passed in a blur, my body moving almost on autopilot. As the miles accumulated, fatigue set in, but the thought of crossing the finish line kept me going. The support from spectators, the high-fives from fellow runners, and the encouragement from my family and friends helped me push through the tough moments. The final stretch was the hardest; my legs felt like they were lead, and every step was a struggle. But as I saw the finish line in the distance, a surge of energy propelled me forward.

Crossing the finish line was a moment of pure triumph. The weight of the medal around my neck was a tangible reminder of the hard work, dedication, and perseverance that had brought me to this point. The sense of pride and accomplishment was overwhelming. It wasn't just about finishing the race; it was about proving to myself that I could set and achieve a challenging goal. The experience transformed my perspective on what was possible, not just in running, but in life. It inspired others around me, showing that it's never too late to take on new challenges and push beyond perceived limits.

The marathon experience also had a ripple effect on my life. I continued to run, joining more races and setting new goals. The discipline and dedication required for marathon training spilled over into other areas of my life, enhancing my overall well-being. I found myself more focused, more resilient, and more confident. The friendships formed during training deepened, creating a supportive community beyond running. We celebrated each other's achievements, shared in each other's struggles, and found joy in the simple act of running together.

The journey from that first conversation with Susan to crossing the finish line was filled with challenges and moments of joy, connection, and self-discovery. It taught me that we are capable of so much more than we often realize and that pursuing a challenging goal can bring profound fulfillment and growth.

8.3 A GRANDMOTHER'S FIRST COMPUTER CLASS

Technology had always seemed like a foreign language to her. With their gadgets and apps, her grandchildren easily moved through the digital world while she felt left behind. The day she decided to take a computer class was a turning point. She wanted to stay connected with her family and friends and understand the world they were so immersed in. The decision was filled with apprehension but also determination. The thought of video chatting with distant relatives or sharing photos online was enough to motivate her.

Walking into the first computer class, she felt excitement and nervousness. The room was filled with others like her, eager to learn but unsure where to start. The instructor, Alex, a kind and patient young man, welcomed them with a reassuring smile. He started with the basics, explaining the parts of a computer and how to use a mouse and keyboard. It was initially overwhelming, but Alex's step-by-step approach made it manageable. Each lesson built on the previous one, and slowly, her confidence grew. She spent hours practicing at home, navigating the internet, and using different software. There were moments of frustration when things didn't work as expected or she got confused, but she kept going, determined to master these new skills.

The support from her family was invaluable. Her grandchildren were thrilled to help, often sitting with her and explaining things in simple terms. They showed her how to use social media, set up an email account, and even introduced her to online games. Their patience and encouragement made the learning process enjoyable. Her classmates also became a source of support. They shared tips, celebrated each other's progress, and bonded over their shared experiences. The sense of community in the class was uplifting, making the learning journey less daunting.

Milestones came one after another, each one a victory. Sending that first email was exhilarating, a simple act that opened up a world of communication. Video chatting with relatives was a highlight, seeing their faces and hearing their voices made the distance seem smaller. Creating a social media account was another milestone. She reconnected with old friends, shared photos and updates, and felt more engaged with the world. Discovering online resources for her hobbies, like cooking and gardening tutorials, added another layer of enjoyment. Each achievement boosted her confidence and made her feel more connected.

The impact of her new skills was profound. The confidence she gained extended beyond the digital world. She felt more independent and more capable of navigating the modern world. The ability to stay connected with loved ones enriched her relationships, bridging the gap that technology once represented. Her experience also inspired others. Friends who had been hesitant to embrace technology saw her progress and decided to take classes themselves. The sense of empowerment that came with learning something new at her age was incredibly fulfilling.

It reminded me that it's never too late to embrace change, learn, and grow.

8.4 THE HOME RENOVATION PROJECT

The idea of renovating our family home had been on my mind for years. The house, filled with memories and love, needed updates to suit our modern lifestyle. Watching home improvement shows and flipping through magazines inspired me to take on the project. It wasn't just about aesthetics but about creating a space that reflected our evolving needs and tastes. The decision to renovate was exciting and daunting, but our vision of a transformed home motivated us.

Planning was the first step. We sat down to create a detailed renovation plan and budget, outlining our goals and priorities. The process of deciding on designs, materials, and layouts was both fun and challenging. We wanted to preserve the character of the house while incorporating modern elements. Once the plan was set, we began the execution phase. The initial stages involved clearing out rooms and preparing for construction. It was chaotic, with unexpected issues like structural repairs cropping up. Navigating these challenges required patience and flexibility, but overcoming each obstacle brought us closer to our dream home.

The renovation project was a team effort. Family members pitched in with DIY projects like painting and assembling furniture. Even the grandchildren got involved, helping with small tasks and learning valuable skills along the way. Working closely with contractors, we ensured that the quality of work met our expectations. The collaboration and teamwork made the process more enjoyable, turning it into a bonding experience. We celebrated each milestone, from installing new kitchen cabinets to completing the garden patio, with small gatherings and shared meals.

The day the renovation was completed was a moment of sheer satisfaction. We hosted a housewarming party and invited friends and family to see the transformed space. The joy and pride we felt as we walked them through each room were indescribable. The updated home was not just beautiful; it was functional and reflective of our tastes and needs. Each corner held a story, a memory of the effort and love that went into the project. Enjoying the new space, whether cooking in the modern kitchen or relaxing in the redesigned living room, brought a sense of accomplishment and contentment. The renovation project was more than just a home makeover; it was a testament to our creativity, determination, and the power of working together as a family.

Reflection section: Think of moments in your life when you overcame a hurdle that seemed impossible to overcome. Do you remember what made you do it, and how did the personal victory feel for you? If the memory of that victory feels good, celebrate it again! Why not?

9

PETS AND ANIMALS

When I was a child, our family had a golden retriever named Max. Max wasn't just a pet; he was a family member. Every morning, he would wait by the door, his tail wagging furiously as soon as he heard the first footsteps. He'd follow us around the house, always eager to participate in whatever we were doing. His loyalty was unwavering. On days when I felt down, Max seemed to understand. He'd lay his head on my lap, his eyes full of empathy, offering silent comfort that words couldn't provide.

9.1 THE LOYAL DOG

Dogs have an incredible way of connecting with us on a deep emotional level. Their loyalty is something truly remarkable. Imagine coming home after a long day, feeling exhausted and worn out. As soon as you open the door, your furry friend eagerly awaits. His tail wags so hard it seems like his whole body is moving. He jumps up, his eyes shining joyfully as if he's been waiting for this moment all day. That pure, unfiltered happiness is contagious. It lifts your spirits and makes you feel good.

Beyond the everyday joy they bring, dogs provide emotional support in ways that can be life-changing. During difficult times, their presence offers a unique kind of comfort. I remember when a dear friend went through a tough battle with illness. Her dog, Bella, never left her side. Bella seemed to sense when her owner was in pain or feeling low. She would curl up next to her, providing warmth and companionship that no medicine could match.

It's been shown that Emotional Support Animals (ESAs) can significantly impact mental health. For instance, a young woman named Anna Walters used her ESA dog, Muffins, to cope with Generalized Anxiety Disorder (GAD) triggered by her parents' divorce. Muffins provided the stability and comfort Anna needed to manage her anxiety and navigate through a challenging period.

Dogs are also there for us during moments of stress. Whether it's the pressure of a big event or the burden of daily worries, their calming presence can make a world of difference. I think back to a time when work stress had me feeling overwhelmed. My dog, Rusty, would sit by my feet as I worked late into the night. Just having him there, his steady breathing and occasional nudge for attention, helped me stay grounded. He reminded me to take breaks and reconnect with the simple joys of life.

The adventures and activities shared with dogs create some of the most memorable moments. Daily walks become cherished routines. Exploring new trails together turns into mini-adventures. I loved taking Rusty to the local park, where he would run free, chasing after sticks and playing fetch. His joy was infectious, and those moments brought a sense of freedom and connection to nature. Each walk was a new opportunity to bond, to share in the simple pleasure of being outdoors and enjoying each other's company.

Celebrating a dog's birthday might seem trivial to some, but it's a special occasion for dog owners. I remember baking a dog-friendly cake for Max's tenth birthday. We threw a little party in the backyard, complete with party hats and treats. Max's tail wagged non-stop as he enjoyed his cake and the extra attention. It was a day filled with laughter and love, a testament to the joy he brought into our lives. These celebrations are more than just fun; they're a way to honor the bond we share with our pets.

Over the years, dogs leave an indelible mark on our hearts. Their playful antics and unique personalities become cherished memories. I often remember Max's and Rusty's quirks, like how they would tilt their heads when they heard a strange noise or their love for chasing squirrels. These memories are a source of comfort and joy, a reminder of our special bond. The loyalty, companionship, and unconditional love of dogs enrich our lives in ways that are hard to put into words. They teach us patience, empathy, and the importance of living in the moment.

Reflection Section

Think about a dog or other pet that has been special in your life. Take a moment to reflect on the bond you shared and the memories you created together. Consider jotting down a few of these memories in a journal. What were some of their unique quirks? How did they provide comfort during tough times? What activities did you enjoy together? Reflecting on these moments can bring a sense of gratitude and joy, celebrating our loyal companions' lasting impact on our lives.

9.2 CAT CUDDLES

There's something incredibly soothing about the presence of a cat. Imagine a quiet evening at home, the soft purring of your feline companion as it curls up on your lap. The rhythmic sound is like a gentle lullaby, easing away the day's stresses. The cat's body warms your lap, and you feel a sense of peace and contentment. The gentle kneading of its paws as it settles in for a nap is comforting and endearing. This simple act, often called "making biscuits," is a throwback to kittenhood and a sign of deep relaxation and trust. It's moments like these that make you appreciate a cat's quiet, calming presence.

Cats are known for their playful and quirky behaviors, which never fail to bring joy and amusement. You've likely seen your cat go into a frenzy, chasing after a laser pointer or a feather toy. Their agility and speed are impressive, and their antics can be downright hilarious. One minute, they're stalking the elusive red dot and the next, they're pouncing with all their might. And then, there are the times when they get into mischief, knocking objects off shelves with a casual swat of their paw. It's as if they're testing the laws of gravity, one trinket at a time. These playful moments remind you of the joy found in simple pleasures and the importance of taking time to play.

The bond between cats and their owners is truly special. There's a unique language of love and connection that develops over time. A cat rubbing against your legs is a sign of affection, a way of marking you as theirs. It's a gesture that says, "You belong to me." These moments of connection are precious, whether sharing quiet moments together while reading a book or watching TV. Cats can make themselves comfortable, often curling up next to you or finding a cozy spot on your lap. Their presence is a reminder of companionship and the comfort of having a loyal friend by your side.

Cats show independence and have distinct personalities. Each cat has its favorite hiding spots and routines. Maybe your cat loves to perch on the windowsill, watching the world go by. Or perhaps it has a secret nook where it likes to retreat for some quiet time.

Cats communicate their needs and desires through a variety of meows, purrs, and body language. A slow blink from a cat is a sign of trust and affection, while a gentle head-butt is a way of saying hello. Understanding these signals deepens the bond between you and your feline friend, creating a relationship built on mutual respect and love.

I remember my cat, Milo, who had a penchant for hiding in the most unexpected places. One day, after searching high and low, I found him nestled inside a laundry basket, his green eyes peering out from a pile of clothes. It was his little sanctuary, a place where he felt safe and hidden.

He had a unique way of letting me know when he wanted attention. He would sit at my feet, staring up at me with those big eyes, and let out a soft, insistent meow. It was impossible to ignore, and I would scoop him up, feeling his warm body relax against mine as he purred contentedly.

Sharing your life with a cat brings a deep sense of fulfillment and joy. Their soothing presence, playful antics, and unique personalities enrich your daily routine. Whether it's the comfort of a cat purring softly on your lap, the laughter from their playful behaviors, or the special bond you share, cats make life a little brighter and a lot more interesting. They remind you to slow down, enjoy the moment, and appreciate the simple pleasures in life.

9.3 HORSEBACK ADVENTURES

The connection between a horse and its rider is a unique bond built on trust and mutual respect. It starts long before you ever mount the saddle. Picture this: you're in the stable, the earthy scent of hay filling the air as you approach your horse. You begin the process of grooming, running a brush through its coat, feeling the warmth and strength beneath your fingers. It's a ritual that calms you and the horse, a moment of quiet connection. You communicate through gentle touches and soft words as you tack up, securing the saddle and bridle. Your horse responds with quiet understanding, a flick of the ear, or a nuzzle, signaling readiness and trust.

When you finally mount, the world opens up in a way that's hard to describe. Riding through scenic trails, you feel a sense of freedom and adventure. The rhythmic motion of the horse beneath you, the sound of hooves on the ground, and the wind in your face create a symphony of sensory experiences. Open fields stretch out before you, inviting exploration. Whether trotting through a forest path or galloping across a meadow, the connection with your horse deepens. It's a partnership, each of you relying on the other, communicating through subtle shifts in weight and gentle tugs on the reins. These moments of exploration and adventure are more than just rides; they're shared experiences that build a strong, unspoken bond between you and your horse.

Participating in equestrian events and competitions adds another layer of joy and excitement. The thrill of entering the arena, the sense of anticipation and focus, and the exhilaration of performing together as a team are unmatched. Whether it's a dressage test, a jumping course, or a trail competition, the trust and communication you've built with your horse shine through. Each event is a testament to the hours of practice, the dedication, and the love you've poured into this partnership. Winning a ribbon or simply completing a challenging course brings a sense of accomplishment and pride, not just in yourself but in your horse as well.

Horses offer more than just companionship and adventure; they provide therapeutic benefits that can be life-changing. Equine-assisted therapy is a powerful tool for physical and emotional rehabilitation. Spending time with horses, caring for them, and riding can have a calming effect, reducing stress and anxiety. The stable becomes a sanctuary, where worries fade away, replaced by the simple, grounding tasks of feeding, grooming, and mucking out stalls. The repetitive, rhythmic movements of grooming and riding can soothe the mind, providing a sense of peace and stability.

Therapeutic riding can improve balance, coordination, and strength for those facing physical challenges, fostering a sense of independence and achievement.

One of the most rewarding aspects of horseback riding is witnessing the growth and progress of your horse over time. The daily routines of feeding, grooming, and exercising become opportunities to build trust and deepen your bond. You notice the small changes—how your horse becomes more responsive, how its coat shines a little brighter, how it seems to anticipate your next move. These moments of progress, whether it's mastering a new skill or simply becoming more comfortable together, bring immense joy and satisfaction. The commitment and dedication involved in caring for horses are significant, but the rewards are equally profound. Each day spent with your horse is filled with love, learning, and connection.

The commitment to horse care extends beyond the rides and adventures. It's in the everyday tasks, the early mornings, and the late nights. Feeding your horse, ensuring it has fresh water, and maintaining its health are acts of love and responsibility. The joy of seeing your horse thrive, of knowing that your care and attention contribute to its well-being, is deeply rewarding. Horses teach us about patience, empathy, strength, and the importance of consistency. They remind us to be present, to listen, and to appreciate the beauty of simple moments.

9.4 BIRDSONG AND SERENITY

There's a particular joy that comes from waking up to the melodic songs of birds in your garden. Their chirping is like nature's symphony, a gentle reminder that life surrounds us. You might be sipping your morning coffee and watching birds flit between trees and feeders. Seeing a bright red cardinal perched on a branch or a blue jay with its striking plumage darting through the air adds a splash of color to the day. These moments of peaceful observation bring a sense of calm and joy, grounding us in the present.

Birds are incredibly diverse, each species boasting its unique characteristics. And then to think they are the last living descendants of the class of dinosaurs. Take the cardinal, for example. Its vibrant red feathers stand out against the green backdrop of trees, making it a delight to spot. Blue jays are equally captivating with their bold blue and white plumage. Their loud calls add a lively soundtrack to the garden. Then, there are the intricate nests built by different bird species. Some birds, like the weaver bird, create elaborate woven nests that are true works of art. Watching these birds as they meticulously construct their homes is a testament to the ingenuity and skill found in nature.

Birdwatching as a hobby offers both excitement and fulfillment. There's something thrilling about spotting a new bird species and adding it to your birdwatching journal. Noting down sightings and behaviors helps you remember these special encounters. You can identify new species and learn more about their habits and habitats using binoculars and bird guides. This hobby keeps your mind sharp and engaged as you continuously learn and discover more about the avian world.

Birds play a crucial role in the natural environment. They act as pollinators, spreading pollen from one flower to another, which helps plants reproduce. Birds like hummingbirds and insects like bees are essential for the health of many ecosystems. They are also seed dispersers, carrying seeds to new locations and thus allowing plants to grow in different areas. This process helps maintain the balance and diversity of plant life.

Seasonal migrations of birds are another fascinating aspect. Countless bird species travel thousands of miles each year to find suitable breeding and feeding grounds. These migrations are vital for their survival and offer incredible spectacles for birdwatchers.

Birdwatching doesn't always require trekking through forests or parks. Sometimes, the best birdwatching happens right in your backyard. Setting up feeders and birdbaths attracts a variety of species, providing endless entertainment and joy. You'll notice how different birds have different feeding habits. Some prefer seeds, while others go for fruits or insects. Each visit to the feeder becomes an opportunity to observe and learn. Filling a feeder and watching the birds that come to enjoy it fosters a connection to nature and a sense of responsibility for its well-being.

One of my favorite birdwatching memories involves an early morning walk in a local park. The air was cool, and the sun had just begun to rise. As I strolled along a wooded path, I heard the distinctive call of a woodpecker. I paused, scanning the trees until I spotted it—a magnificent pileated woodpecker, its bright red crest standing out against the bark. I watched in awe as it pecked at the tree, searching for insects. Moments like these, where you witness the beauty and behavior of birds up close, stay with you and deepen your love for birdwatching.

Birdwatching can also be a social activity. Joining a birdwatching group or going on guided birdwatching tours introduces you to fellow enthusiasts. Sharing sightings and experiences create a sense of community and camaraderie. It's a beautiful way to meet new people who share your interests and to learn from more experienced birdwatchers. These social interactions add another layer of enjoyment to the hobby, making it a rich and fulfilling experience.

The calming effect of birds and their songs, the thrill of identifying new species, and the knowledge that birds play a vital role in ecosystems all contribute to the joy of birdwatching. It's a hobby that fosters a connection to nature and provides endless opportunities for learning and discovery.

Whether you're a seasoned birdwatcher or just starting out, the world of birds offers something for everyone. Birds enrich our lives with their presence and remind us of the beauty and wonder of the natural world.

10

MEMORABLE TRAVEL EXPERIENCES

There's something incredibly thrilling about the open road, the hum of the tires on the pavement, and the promise of adventure just beyond the horizon. I remember one such trip vividly—a road trip to the Grand Canyon. It all began with a spark of an idea, a yearning to see one of nature's greatest wonders. The idea quickly became a family plan, filled with excitement and meticulous preparation.

10.1 THE ROAD TRIP TO THE GRAND CANYON

Preparing for a road trip is almost as exciting as the journey itself. We gathered around the kitchen table, maps sprawled before us, and began plotting our route. The anticipation built as we planned each stop, imagining the quirky roadside attractions and small towns we'd encounter. Packing the car was a family affair. We loaded camping gear, snacks, and essentials, each item carefully chosen to ensure we were ready for anything. The trunk was a puzzle of sleeping bags, coolers, and backpacks, each piece fitting perfectly into place. As we packed, conversations buzzed with excitement about the adventures that awaited us. We talked about the hikes we'd take, the sunsets we'd witness, and the stars we'd gaze at from our campsite. The air was thick with anticipation, and the promise of the open road filled us with a sense of freedom.

The journey through the vast desert landscapes of the Southwest was breathtaking. The scenery changed with every mile, from flat plains to rugged canyons, each landscape more stunning than the last. We drove through small towns that seemed frozen in time, their main streets lined with diners and antique shops. Each stop allowed us to stretch our legs and soak in the local charm. One memorable stop was at a quirky roadside attraction—a giant metal dinosaur standing guard over a small gift shop. We couldn't resist taking photos and browsing the shelves filled with trinkets and souvenirs. The desert stretched out around us, its seemingly endless expanse dotted with cacti and scrub brush. The sky was a brilliant blue, and the sun cast a golden glow over the landscape, making everything feel almost surreal.

As we neared the Grand Canyon, the scenery became even more dramatic. The flat plains gave way to rugged canyons, their red and orange hues glowing in the late afternoon sun. The anticipation grew with each passing mile, and the excitement was palpable. When we finally arrived, the first view of the canyon took our breath away. We reached the Grand Canyon as the sun rose, casting a warm, golden light over the vast expanse. The canyon stretched out before us, its sheer size and beauty overwhelming. We stood in awe, taking in the layers of rock and the deep shadows that shifted with the changing light. The sunrise painted the sky with pink, orange, and purple hues, creating a stunning backdrop to the natural wonder. It was a moment of pure wonder, a reminder of the incredible beauty of the natural world.

Hiking along the rim of the Grand Canyon was an experience like no other. Each step offered a new perspective, a different angle from which to appreciate the canyon's grandeur. The trails wound along the edge, providing panoramic vistas that seemed to stretch on forever. We stopped frequently to take photos, capturing the beauty and the sense of scale that is impossible to convey in words. The air was crisp and clear, and the silence was broken only by a bird's occasional call or the wind's rustle through the trees. It was a peaceful and awe-inspiring journey that brought us closer to nature and each other.

Visiting the Visitor Center was an educational and enriching experience. We learned about the canyon's history and geology, gaining a deeper appreciation for the forces that shaped this incredible landscape. The exhibits were fascinating, providing insights into the flora and fauna that call the canyon home. We marveled at the stories of the early explorers who ventured into the canyon, their courage and determination inspiring us. The knowledge we gained added another layer of wonder to our visit, making the experience even more meaningful.

The sense of accomplishment from completing the road trip was profound. We journeyed through diverse landscapes, encountered new experiences, and witnessed one of the world's greatest natural wonders. The memories of the shared adventure became cherished family stories, retold around the dinner table and at family gatherings. The trip inspired us to plan future road trips, each one an opportunity to explore more natural wonders and create new memories.

10.2 A TRAIN RIDE ACROSS EUROPE

There's a unique charm to exploring Europe by train that's hard to resist. The idea of gliding through diverse landscapes, hopping from one country to another without the hassle of airports, sparked excitement and curiosity. We decided to take the plunge, planning a journey to take us through Europe's heart. The anticipation of visiting multiple countries with distinct cultures, languages, and characters was thrilling. We imagined ourselves sipping coffee in Paris, wandering through the historic streets of Rome, and gazing at the snow-capped peaks of the Swiss Alps.

Our first leg of the trip took us through the scenic countryside of France. As the train sped away from the bustling city of Paris, the landscape transformed into a tapestry of rolling hills and verdant vineyards. The vineyards of Bordeaux stretched out endlessly, their neat rows of grapevines basking in the golden sunlight. The gentle rhythm of the train allowed us to soak in the beauty around us, the fields dotted with charming stone houses and the occasional chateau. We felt a sense of tranquility, a welcome change from the hustle of city life.

Italy was next on our itinerary, and it did not disappoint. The train journey from Milan to Rome was a feast for the eyes, with picturesque villages and ancient ruins dotting the landscape. Rome greeted us with its timeless grandeur. We spent our days wandering through the Colosseum, the Roman Forum, and the Vatican, marveling at the layers of history that seemed to whisper from every stone. Florence, with its Renaissance art and architecture, was equally captivating. The city's narrow streets and bustling piazzas were filled with the sound of street musicians, the aroma of freshly baked bread, and the vibrant energy of locals and tourists alike.

Switzerland was a dream come true for nature lovers. The train journey through the Swiss Alps was nothing short of magical. As we wound through the towering peaks, the landscape shifted from lush green valleys to snow-covered mountains. The sight of quaint villages nestled in the valleys, with wooden chalets and church spires, was like something out of a storybook. We couldn't help but be enchanted by the pristine beauty of the Swiss countryside. The air was crisp and fresh, and the views from the train windows were breathtaking, each scene more stunning than the last.

One of the most memorable aspects of our train journey was the people we met. In the dining car, we struck up conversations with fellow travelers from all over the world. A retired couple from Canada shared stories of their travels, a young backpacker from Australia full of enthusiasm, and a local French artist who spoke passionately about his work. These interactions added a rich layer to our experience, reminding us of the shared humanity that connects us all, no matter where we come from.

Exploring local markets was another highlight of our trip. In France, we wandered through a bustling market in Provence, sampling fresh cheeses, olives, and pastries. In Italy, we visited the

Mercato Centrale in Florence, where the vibrant stalls offered everything from handmade pasta to exotic spices. The colors, smells, and tastes of these markets were a feast for the senses, and we relished the opportunity to immerse ourselves in the local culture. Each market visit was a culinary adventure, a chance to savor the unique flavors of each region.

Our journey took us to historic landmarks that left us in awe. The Eiffel Tower glistened against the night sky in Paris, while the Louvre beckoned with its treasures. Rome's ancient ruins transported us back in time, while Florence's art galleries showcased masterpieces that left us speechless. Switzerland's medieval castles stood as silent sentinels, guarding their secrets. Each landmark told its own story, deepening our appreciation for Europe's rich history and cultural heritage.

The train journey across Europe sparked a sense of wonder and curiosity that stayed with us long after we returned home. The diverse experiences, from the serene countryside of France to the historic splendor of Italy and the natural beauty of Switzerland, opened our eyes to the myriad ways people live and celebrate life. The friendships we made along the way, with fellow travelers and locals alike, created a sense of global connectedness that was deeply fulfilling. This adventure inspired us to continue exploring and appreciating different cultures, knowing that there is always something new to discover just around the corner.

10.3 THE CRUISE TO THE CARIBBEAN

Picture this: you arrive at the bustling port, your suitcase in tow, and your heart pounding with excitement. The sheer size of the cruise ship before you is awe-inspiring, a floating city ready to whisk you away on an adventure. The air is filled with the hum of anticipation as fellow travelers mill about, their faces reflecting the same eager anticipation you feel. Boarding the ship feels like stepping into another world. The crew greets you warmly, and you can't help but marvel at the grandeur of the atrium with its sparkling chandeliers and polished marble floors. The promise of fun and relaxation is palpable.

As you explore the ship, the array of amenities and activities leaves you spoiled for choice. There are pools and hot tubs, perfect for a leisurely dip or a relaxing soak. The fitness center beckons those looking to stay active, while the spa offers a sanctuary of tranquility with its soothing treatments. You discover a range of dining options, from elegant restaurants serving gourmet meals to casual eateries offering comfort food. Each corner of the ship holds a new delight, from theaters showcasing dazzling performances to lounges where you can sip cocktails and enjoy live music. The anticipation of the journey ahead fills you with joy and freedom.

The first stop is the Bahamas, and as you disembark, the sight of crystal-clear waters and white sandy beaches takes your breath away. You can't resist the urge to kick off your shoes and feel the soft sand between your toes. The water is inviting, a perfect shade of turquoise that promises refreshment and adventure. You spend the day basking in the sun, swimming in the gentle waves, and exploring the vibrant marine life. Snorkeling in the coral reefs of the Cayman Islands is an experience you'll never forget. The underwater world is a riot of colors, with schools of fish darting among the coral formations. It's like swimming in a giant aquarium, each moment filled with wonder.

In Jamaica, the lush rainforests and cascading waterfalls starkly contrast the serene beaches. You embark on a hike through the tropical landscape, the air thick with the scent of exotic flowers and the sounds of wildlife. The trail leads you to a hidden waterfall, its cool waters inviting you to take a refreshing dip. The beauty of the natural surroundings is mesmerizing, a reminder of the incredible diversity of the Caribbean islands. Each island offers its unique charm, from the bustling markets filled with vibrant crafts and fresh produce to the historic sites that tell stories of the past.

One evening, you attend a lively onboard show, the theater filled with anticipation. The performers take the stage, their energy and talent electrifying the audience. It's a dazzling display of music, dance, and acrobatics, each act more impressive than the last. After the show, you head to a themed dinner; the dining room transformed into a festive wonderland. The food is exquisite, each dish a culinary masterpiece tantalizing your taste buds. You find yourself chatting with fellow passengers, sharing stories and laughter, making the evening even more enjoyable.

The friendships you form on the ship add another layer of richness to the experience. You meet a couple celebrating their anniversary, and their love story is inspiring and heartwarming. Over dinner, you share travel tales and dreams of future adventures. On a shore excursion, you visit a historic site, the guide's stories bringing the past to life. You explore local markets, the vibrant atmosphere filled with the sounds of haggling and the rich aroma of spices. Each interaction deepens your appreciation for the journey, creating memories that will last a lifetime.

The sense of relaxation and adventure throughout the cruise is unparalleled—no busy airports, highways, or train stations to worry about. You wake up every morning while the ship has traveled with you to a new island. Each day brings new experiences, from the thrill of discovering a secluded beach to the simple pleasure of watching the sunset from the deck. The rejuvenation you feel is profound, a blend of rest and excitement that leaves you feeling refreshed and invigorated. The shared moments of joy and discovery become cherished family stories, retold with fondness and laughter. The cruise inspires you to plan future voyages, each one a new opportunity to explore the world by sea and create more unforgettable memories.

10.4 VISITING THE ANCESTRAL HOMELAND

Tracing your family roots and deciding to visit the ancestral homeland is a deeply meaningful journey. The excitement and anticipation of discovering family history and connecting with your heritage can be overwhelming. You start by gathering old photographs, letters, and family records, piecing together the puzzle of your lineage. The decision to travel back in time and walk in the footsteps of your ancestors fills you with a sense of purpose. You imagine the stories waiting to be uncovered, the connections to be made, and the traditions to be embraced. This journey is not just a trip; it's a quest to understand where you come from and to honor those who came before you.

The moment you set foot in the village where your ancestors lived, you feel an inexplicable sense of belonging. The narrow cobblestone streets, the quaint houses with their flower-filled window boxes, and the church bell tolling in the distance all seem strangely familiar. You visit the local church where generations of your family were baptized, married, and laid to rest. The historic sites and landmarks related to your family history come alive as you explore them. Each stone and each path tells a story, connecting you to your roots in a way you never imagined. You walk through the town square, imagining your great-grandparents doing the same, their lives intertwined with the very fabric of this place.

Meeting distant relatives is one of the most enriching parts of this journey. People who have only heard of you through family stories welcome you with open arms. They share their lives and traditions with you, making you feel like a part of their world. You sit around a long wooden table, sharing a meal from recipes passed down through generations. Laughter and conversation flow easily, bridging the gap of time and distance. The bonds you form with these relatives are immediate and profound, rooted in the shared history you all cherish. You listen to their stories, learn about their struggles and triumphs, and realize that these tales are part of your heritage.

One of the most memorable experiences is discovering old family records and heirlooms. In a dusty attic or an old chest, you find birth certificates, marriage licenses, and letters written in a delicate, looping script. These documents are tangible links to your past, providing insights into the lives of your ancestors. You uncover a family Bible with handwritten notes in the margins, chronicling births, deaths, and marriages over centuries. Each discovery feels like a treasure, a piece of your family's history brought to light. You hold these objects with reverence, knowing that they have been touched by the hands of those who came before you.

Participating in local customs and traditions gives you a deeper understanding of your heritage. You join the village festival, dancing to traditional music and tasting dishes prepared the same way for generations. You learn to make bread using an old family recipe, and the kitchen is filled with the comforting aroma of baking. You visit the local craftspeople, watching them create works of art using techniques passed down through the ages. These experiences are more than just activities; they are a way to connect with your ancestors on a visceral level. You feel a sense of pride and fulfillment as you embrace these traditions, knowing that you are keeping them alive.

Walking in the footsteps of your ancestors is an emotional experience. You stand on the same ground they once walked, seeing the world through their eyes. The connection you feel to them is profound, a bond that transcends time. You visit the gravesites of your forebears, laying flowers and saying a quiet prayer. The sense of loss and longing is tempered by the knowledge that you are part of a continuous line of life, a thread woven into the tapestry of your family's history. This journey is not just about discovering your past; it's about understanding who you are and where you come from.

The lasting impact of this trip is immeasurable. You return home with a deepened understanding and appreciation of your family heritage. The stories and traditions you encountered become a part of your life, enriching it in ways you never thought possible. You feel a sense of pride and fulfillment from connecting with your roots, knowing that you are part of something larger than yourself. This journey inspires you to preserve and share your family history with future generations, ensuring that the legacy of your ancestors lives on. The connections you made, the stories you heard, and the traditions you embraced become a cherished part of your own story, a testament to the enduring power of family and heritage.

CONCLUSION

As we end our journey together, I want to thank you for joining me in exploring the wonderful world of shared memories, love, and laughter. This book was written to bring us closer, reminisce about the moments that have shaped our lives, and celebrate the joy we find in the simple things.

From the very beginning, in **Chapter 1**, we delved into **Family and Relationships**. We shared stories of grandparents' love, cherished family quilts, and the enduring bonds of siblings and parents. These tales remind us of the warmth and wisdom that family brings into our lives.

Then, in **Chapter 2**, we reflected on **Historical Moments**. Remember the moon landing watch parties, the magic of Woodstock, and the fall of the Berlin Wall? These events didn't just shape the world—they shaped our personal histories and brought us together in times of awe and change.

We then moved to **Chapter 3**, where we embraced **Nature and the Outdoors**. Whether it was the majesty of national parks, the serenity of stargazing, or the simple pleasure of walking through autumn woods, we explored how nature offers us peace and a reminder of life's beauty.

In **Chapter 4**, we celebrated **Love and Gratitude**. Stories of enduring love, acts of kindness, and the joy of giving highlighted how these simple gestures make our lives richer and more meaningful.

Chapter 5 brought us back to **Simple Pleasures**. Morning coffee rituals, porch swing conversations, and the charm of old movies remind us to savor the everyday joys that bring comfort and contentment.

In **Chapter 6**, we explored the strength of **Community and Friendship**. Whether gathering at the local diner, reuniting with old friends, or volunteering together, these stories showcased the power of human connection and support.

Chapter 7 explored cultural traditions, celebrating diverse customs, from Christmas around the world to harvest festivals. These traditions connect us to our roots and enrich our lives with a sense of heritage and belonging.

In **Chapter 8**, we shared **Personal Triumphs**. We saw how overcoming fears, like learning to swim at sixty-two or running a marathon, can transform our lives and inspire us to keep pushing boundaries.

We then turned to our furry and feathered friends in **Chapter 9** with **Pets and Animals**. Stories of loyal dogs, cuddly cats, and the joy of birdwatching remind us of the unconditional love and companionship animals bring into our lives.

Finally, in **Chapter 10**, we embarked on **Memorable Travel Experiences**. Road trips to the Grand Canyon, train rides across

Europe, cruising the Caribbean, and visits to ancestral homelands showed us how travel broadens our horizons and creates lasting memories.

Key Takeaways: These chapters have shown how the simplest moments often hold the most profound joy. Whether it's a shared cup of coffee, a walk in the woods, or a heartfelt letter, these small acts connect us to each other and to the world around us.

Call-to-Action: I encourage you to reflect on your own memories and experiences. Share your stories with loved ones, revisit cherished traditions, and embrace the simple pleasures that bring you joy. Reach out to old friends, explore new places, and never stop learning and growing.

Personal Note from the Author: Writing this book has been a journey of reflection and gratitude for me. Being forced into early retirement turned out to be a blessing in disguise. It allowed me to see life from a different perspective and appreciate the little things that truly matter. I am grateful for the opportunity to share these stories with you and hope they have brought a smile to your face and warmth to your heart.

Future Invitations: This is not the end but rather a new beginning. Let's continue to share our stories and experiences. I invite you to join me in future endeavors, whether it's through writing, sharing memories, or exploring new adventures. Our journey through life is enriched by the connections we make and the stories we tell.

Thank you for taking this journey with me. May your days be filled with memorable moments, love, and laughter. Here's to celebrating the past and embracing the future together!

PLEASE TAKE A MOMENT TO LEAVE A REVIEW ON AMAZON.

I hope you enjoyed reading my book.

Please don't leave without leaving a review!

Your opinion matters...

Your help is essential so others find this book and benefit from it, too.

As a self-published author, your feedback is my lifeline and essential for reaching more people who are looking for books they enjoy.

Please take a moment to leave a review on Amazon.

It's quick and easy:

1. Find the book on Amazon, or even faster click your 'Returns & Orders' button
2. Scroll down and click on "Write a product review."
3. Share your thoughts and click "Submit."

Or, simply scan the QR code below to go straight to the review page.

Thank you for your support and for helping others discover this book!

REFERENCES

- Aberdeen Senior Living. (n.d.). *Bird-watching basics for seniors.* https://www.aberdeenseniorliving.com/post/bird-watching-basics-for-seniors
- American Humane. (n.d.). *Cats & seniors.* https://www.americanhumane.org/fact-sheet/cats-seniors/
- Area Agency on Aging. (2023, July 15). *Neighbors helping neighbors' concept can help older adults.* https://areaagencyonaging.org/generations-columns/neighbors-helping-neighbors-concept-can-help-older-adults-christine-vanlandingham-july-15-2023/
- Britannica. (n.d.). *Golden age of American radio | Definition, shows, & facts.* https://www.britannica.com/topic/Golden-Age-of-American-radio
- Duchess of Disneyland. (n.d.). *Tomorrowland's 1969 moon landing viewing party.* https://duchessofdisneyland.com/park-history/tomorrowlands-1969-moon-landing-viewing-party/
- ESA Care. (n.d.). *More than a pet: 7 heroic emotional support animal stories.* https://esacare.com/7-heroic-emotional-support-animals-stories/
- Fearless Fresh. (n.d.). *A brief history of Christmas cookies.* https://fearlessfresh.com/a-brief-history-of-christmas-cookies/
- Fifth Room. (n.d.). *The history of porch swings.* https://blog.fifthroom.com/the-history-of-the-porch-swing.html
- Folklife Magazine. (n.d.). *Quilts of our mothers: Five generations of family craft.* Smithsonian Folklife. https://folklife.si.edu/magazine/family-quilts-mothers
- Hudson Valley Magazine. (n.d.). *Read firsthand festival accounts from the Woodstock generation.* https://hvmag.com/things-to-do/read-firsthand-festival-accounts-from-the-woodstock-generation/
- Ignite Post. (n.d.). *The psychology of handwritten letters and its impact on relationships.* https://www.ignitepost.com/blog/the-psychology-of-handwritten-letters
- Inspired Living. (n.d.). *The benefits of morning coffee for seniors.* https://www.inspiredliving.care/the-benefits-of-morning-coffee-for-seniors/

- Kiricard. (n.d.). *25+ traditional craft techniques from around the world.* https://kiricard.com/25-traditional-craft-techniques-from-around-the-world/
- Love, T. (n.d.). *Love—guess who! Valentine's letters from World War II.* The National WWII Museum. https://www.nationalww2museum.org/war/articles/valentines-letters-world-war-ii
- McLean Hospital. (n.d.). *The mental health benefits of getting outdoors.* https://www.mcleanhospital.org/essential/nature
- Medicare.org. (n.d.). *Senior computer classes to try online for free.* https://www.medicare.org/articles/senior-computer-classes-to-try-online-for-free/
- Monarch Landing. (n.d.). *The benefits of joining a book club for seniors.* https://www.welcometomonarchlanding.com/blog/book-club-for-seniors/
- My Grand Canyon Park. (n.d.). *6 best Grand Canyon road trips and stops on the way.* https://www.mygrandcanyonpark.com/road-trips/road-trip-itineraries/
- National Geographic. (n.d.). *Top 10 harvest festivals around the world.* https://www.nationalgeographic.com/travel/article/harvest-festivals
- NCBI. (n.d.). *Effects of a therapeutic horseback riding program on children with autism spectrum disorder.* https://www.ncbi.nlm.nih.gov/pmc/articles/PMC7967314/
- NCBI. (n.d.). *The role of grandparents' influence in grandchildren's upbringing.* https://www.ncbi.nlm.nih.gov/pmc/articles/PMC10514349/
- Paper & Diamond. (n.d.). *The amazing health benefits of a seaside vacation.* https://www.paperanddiamond.com/journal/health-benefits-seaside-vacation#:.
- Points Guy. (n.d.). *Caribbean cruise guide: Best itineraries, planning tips and more.* https://thepointsguy.com/cruise/caribbean-cruise-guide/
- Seat61. (n.d.). *Train travel in Europe | A beginner's guide.* https://www.seat61.com/european-train-travel.htm
- Senior Helpers. (n.d.). *The benefits of strong relationships for seniors.* https://www.seniorhelpers.com/ma/south-shore/resources/blogs/the-benefits-of-strong-relationships-for-seniors/
- Senior Helpers. (2023, April 1). *How seniors can benefit from learning new skills and staying engaged.* https://www.seniorhelpers.com/tn/middle-tn/resources/blogs/2023-04-01/
- Smithsonian Media Showcase. (n.d.). *The impact of nostalgic media.*

https://sbmediashowcase.com/2467/studies/the-impact-of-nostalgic-media/#:.
- StoryCorps. (n.d.). *Separated by time and distance, best friends reunited after more than three decades.* https://storycorps.org/stories/separated-by-time-and-distance-best-friends-reunited-after-more-than-three-decades/
- Sustainable Restaurant Association. (n.d.). *Around the modern-day fire: The role of restaurants as community hubs.* https://thesra.org/news-insights/insights/around-the-modern-day-fire-the-role-of-restaurants-as-community-hubs/
- Timeout. (n.d.). *The 15 best places for stargazing in the U.S.* https://www.timeout.com/usa/things-to-do/best-places-to-stargaze-in-us
- U.S. News. (n.d.). *Best U.S. national parks for 2024.* https://travel.usnews.com/rankings/best-national-parks-in-the-usa/
- Vox. (n.d.). *Small acts of kindness matter more than you think.* https://www.vox.com/even-better/23670005/small-acts-kindness-matter-liking-gap
- Week, The. (n.d.). *8 inspiring stories about runners.* https://theweek.com/articles/465263/8-inspiring-stories-about-runners

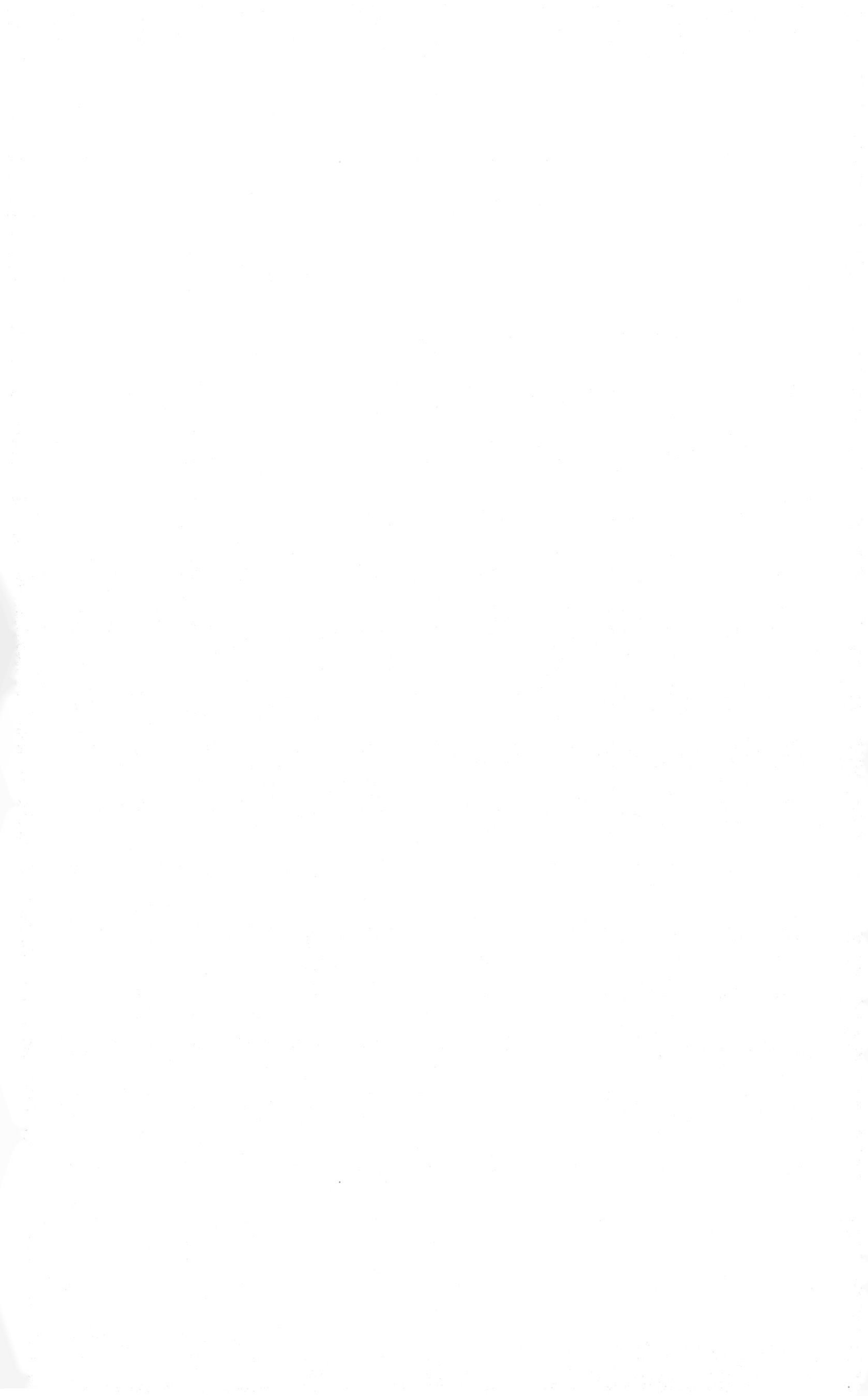

Printed in Great Britain
by Amazon